'Do you alwa... importunate ...

'Only those who w...
Megan said blithely, ...
the corner of the couch.

Lucas's eyes followed her down, lingering to caress the shapely curves of her calves with an intensity which brought a tiny gasp to her lips. She couldn't recall the last time she had experienced such an instantaneous kick of desire.

'Determined to keep all men at arm's length, Red?' Lucas's mocking query pierced her bemusement.

'I reserve the right to choose who I want to have affairs with,' she responded lightly, though in truth her 'affairs' were in the singular. Which could hardly have been said of the man who stood before her.

'Making sure you only choose those men you can control, no doubt,' Lucas remarked coolly. 'What are you afraid of?'

'What are *you* afraid of? You're conspicuously unattached yourself.'

'True, but my method of parting is less Draconian. That poor fool outside bared his soul to you... Where's your compassion?'

'He didn't love me,' she said evenly. 'And even if he did he won't tomorrow.'

Lucas shook his head incredulously. 'How did you get to be so hard?'

Amanda Browning still lives in the Essex house where she was born. The third of four children—her sister being her twin—she enjoyed the rough and tumble of life with two brothers as much as she did reading books. Writing came naturally as an outlet for a fertile imagination. The love of books led her to a career in libraries, and being single allowed her to take the leap into writing for a living. Success is still something of a wonder, but allows her to indulge in hobbies as varied as embroidery and bird-watching.

SEDUCED

BY

AMANDA BROWNING

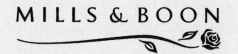

MILLS & BOON

All the characters in this book have no existence outside the imagination of the author, and have no relation whatsoever to anyone bearing the same name or names. They are not even distantly inspired by any individual known or unknown to the author, and all the incidents are pure invention.

*MILLS & BOON and the Rose Device
are trademarks of the publisher.
Harlequin Mills & Boon Limited,
Eton House, 18–24 Paradise Road, Richmond, Surrey TW9 1SR*

© Amanda Browning 1996

ISBN 0 263 79789 9

*Set in 10 on 11 pt Linotron Times
01-9609-59661*

*Typeset in Great Britain by CentraCet, Cambridge
Made and printed in Great Britain*

CHAPTER ONE

MEGAN TERRELL caught the sound of a car driving into the yard and paused in the act of studying the drawings for the only boat currently being built by what had once been a small but thriving company. It had never been unusual for vehicles to come and go at the Terrell boatyard, but they had a tendency, these days, to bear creditors, not potential customers.

Frowning, she wondered if she had forgotten to pay a bill, but was sure she hadn't. Keeping track of their debts bordered on paranoia with her, so that she knew what had to be paid yesterday, and what could wait a little longer. Her stomach clenched. Unless Daniel— She cut off the alarming thought. Don't borrow trouble, their father had always said, and it was doubly valid now, when she had enough of her own to contend with.

'Sounds like visitors. Were you expecting anyone, Ted?' she asked the man who stood beside her. Ted Powell was the genius who turned her designs into the sleek craft Terrell's were renowned for. Once he had had a dozen men working with him, now there were only two. It was sad. She refused to think it was hopeless, however.

He shook his head. 'Not that I can recall, unless the German's changed his mind. It was a beautiful boat, Megan. One of your best,' he added, and she sighed wistfully.

It had been beautiful, and the commission had been worth its weight in gold. Only they couldn't afford to hire more staff, and the German hadn't been prepared to wait. The cancellation had been a blow. Quite

frankly, she had been relying on the commission to tide
them over.

Megan shook her head, knowing better than to hang
onto the slim hope. 'He was pretty adamant,' she
recalled, and pulled a face at the sound of a car door
slamming. 'I'd better go and see who it is. You never
know, it could be somebody wanting us to build a fleet!'
she joked wryly, before hurrying off.

Thank heavens for a sense of humour, she thought
as she approached the door. It was essential in these
days of recession when boats were a luxury most people
had decided they could live without. However, just in
case someone had won the pools and decided to allow
Terrell's to share their good fortune, she pinned a smile
of welcome on her face. With her first glimpse of the
visitor, her eyebrows rose in surprise and her smile
grew crooked. Lucas! The man standing propped
against the wing of his car, dressed in an expensive silk
shirt and casual trousers, was without doubt Lucas
Canfield.

It was eight years since she had seen him in the flesh,
but with the success of his computer empire giving him
millionaire status, and looks a movie star would have
envied, his face was splashed across the papers so often
he was virtually a household name. Like washing-up
liquid, though not as squeaky clean! Her eyes danced
at the analogy, for he had always been unrepentant
about his reputation with the opposite sex. The Lucas
Canfield phenomenon had been a worthy target for her
taunting until he had removed himself from her orbit.

Megan could see what women saw in him. He was as
handsome as sin, and just as darkly seductive. He was
also elusive, as they discovered to their cost. Lucas was
a butterfly, flitting from one woman to the next, sam-
pling each, staying a while before going on to the next
unknown, and perhaps tastier morsel. She'd known it

when she was eighteen and he seven years older. Now he was thirty-three, and nothing had changed.

Right this minute he had his long, muscular legs crossed at the ankles, and his arms folded over his powerful chest in a way she recalled as uniquely his. She'd long ago lost count of the number of times she'd squared up to him when he'd looked as relaxed as this.

At sixteen she had taken it upon herself to improve him, to save him from himself. Her shots could have been made of rubber the way they had bounced off him. She'd get angry, and he would laugh, teasing her about her own romantic ideas of love and marriage. The trouble was, it had been hard to stay angry with him for long. In the end she had given up her attempts, settling for a constant taunting, so that he should never forget that one female wasn't impressed.

She admitted to being impressed now, for he looked tanned and healthy, so vibrantly alive that he charged the air around him. His strongly etched, enticingly handsome face bore little sign of the passing of time, and was still framed by a shock of black hair. Then there were his eyes. Unforgettable eyes of such an intense blue that it would be easy for a woman to drown in them. Many had. The list was endless. And it was all done with so little effort on his part. Oh, yes, he was still Lucas, as rawly masculine as he had ever been.

The sound of feminine laughter distracted her from her study, and she caught her breath as a leggy blonde swayed into view and attached herself to Lucas's arm, hanging on like a limpet whilst he smiled down at her in a way Megan could only describe as lecherous. As she watched, Lucas lowered his head, pressing a lingering kiss to an inviting pair of lips.

Megan felt her smile slip as a small flicker of anger sprung to life, only to be instantly dismissed as her lip curled wryly. She shouldn't be surprised when she had just been thinking of him as the playboy he was. His picture was always in the society pages, and he was never alone. He had been photographed with some of the most beautiful women in the world. She didn't know how he found time to make his money, but he did, because he was as well-known for his corporate activities as he was for his more personal ones.

'How much longer must we wait? There's obviously nobody here, and I'm starving. Don't forget you promised me lunch, Lucas, darling,' the blonde pouted, and Megan got the impression that food wasn't what she was thinking about at all.

However, the interruption reminded her that she couldn't stand skulking in the shadows for ever, with the possibility of Lucas discovering her there. What he would say to that would probably burn her ears off. Their relationship had always been feisty, a kind of private war in which they used whatever weapons came to hand, normally verbal. Truth to tell, she had always kind of enjoyed their fights, even though she'd usually lost, and it occurred to her now that she had actually missed them. Perhaps that was why her heart was beating just a little faster as she prepared to step outside, because she anticipated a very lively exchange.

A tiny smile curved her lips as she moved. Lucas was the first to catch sight of her as she emerged into the sunlight. He straightened immediately, blatantly carrying out a lazy inspection of her person. Surprisingly, she felt the lick of it like a tongue of flame on her flesh, but before she could ponder what it meant he unleashed a smile on her that lit up his deep blue eyes in a way which heralded devilment of some sort, and Megan laughed, shaking her head despairingly. He hadn't changed.

'Hello, stranger,' she greeted him easily, pleased to see him, though she wouldn't boost his ego by saying so.

'Well, well, well, if it isn't little Megan all grown-up at last.'

Megan sent him an old-fashioned look. 'I was grown-up when you last saw me,' she reminded him drily.

'Ah, but you only had the promise of the beauty you've become,' Lucas contested, and, much to her surprise, Megan felt heat sting her cheeks at the fulsome compliment.

She told herself her reaction was simply due to the fact that she didn't expect kind words from him. Insults, yes, compliments, no. 'Stop it, Lucas. You'll be turning my head next!' she rebuked him, grinning.

In the next instant her smile slipped as she saw her brother come out of the office. He wasn't supposed to be here. Only days ago he had gone to a race meeting up north with his friends. Ice trickled down her spine as she computed the possible reasons for Daniel's presence. The logical one would be because he actually owned Terrell's, but logic had nothing to do with his behaviour these days. It was the unpalatable alternative which churned up her stomach. If he was back this early, it probably meant he had run out of money! She didn't need the inevitable argument that that would bring on top of losing a valuable commission.

'Good God, Lucas!' Daniel's stunned exclamation as he recognised the visitor echoed round the yard.

Megan bit back a demand to know what had happened because Lucas was Daniel's friend, and had been from her brother's first day at school, when Lucas, older by two years, had taken it upon himself to make the new boy welcome. It was a bond which had never been broken, and she couldn't jeopardise it with rash words. She would wait until they were alone.

Lucas detached himself from the blonde and moved towards his friend, his eyes and voice amused. 'You look as though you've seen a ghost. Is my turning up like this so unpleasant, Dan?'

Ignoring his sister, whom he must have seen, Daniel
smiled broadly. 'Hell, no!' he denied, grinning delight-
edly, and held out his hand to the man he had hero-
worshipped as a boy. 'It's good to see you, Lucas.
Damn good,' he insisted as Lucas shook the proffered
hand.

Megan watched them going through the back-slap-
ping motions of male bonding, wishing, not for the first
time, that Lucas had not moved away. He had always
been a good influence on her brother. She could have
done with that these last few months when Daniel had
become like a rudderless ship, at the mercy of every
vagrant tide or wind—the very last thing she needed
with the recession damaging the business. Because she
needed Terrell's. It was her anchor, her purpose, and
Daniel was setting it on a direct course for the rocks.

'What took you so long to find your way back here?'
Daniel asked, stuffing his hands into the back pockets
of his jeans. 'Did you lose our address?'

Lucas accepted the criticism with a wry smile. 'I
shouldn't have left it so long, but it's good to see you
too, Dan. And the old place,' he declared warmly,
reacquainting himself with the yard he had known so
well as a boy. 'I have to admit I wasn't sure of finding
you still here. A lot of good companies have gone to
the wall these last few years.'

Daniel's laugh was off-key as he dragged a hand
through his hair, and once again he avoided looking at
Megan. 'Not us, thank God. We're on the crest of a
wave. Things couldn't be better!' he declared, and
Megan's lips twisted bitterly as she heard the outright
lie. Not that she was surprised. Daniel certainly
wouldn't want his idol to know the awful truth.

Lucas nodded. 'I'm glad to hear it, though it wouldn't
have surprised me to hear things were rough,' he
responded, and Megan held her breath, wondering how
her brother would respond to the invitation.

Laughing dismissively, Daniel didn't quite meet his friend's eyes. 'We've been lucky, I guess,' he said, and finally turned to his sister. 'Hi, Meg. Isn't this great? You could have knocked me down with a feather when I saw him!' he exclaimed with an uneasy laugh.

He might well be uneasy, Megan thought acidly. He was hoping that Lucas's arrival would sidetrack her from his own unexpected appearance. She might have said nothing at all if she hadn't seen the flush on his cheeks, and recognised the cause. Daniel had started drinking several months ago, and she hadn't been able to stop him. It was another bone of contention between them.

'I thought you were in York,' she said staunchly, and angry colour rose up his neck.

'Not now, for God's sake, Meg!' he snapped, glaring at her, and she knew her assumptions about the early return were correct. Fortunately for him, she had no intention of airing their dirty linen in public, but she would not let it pass unacknowledged.

'Well, since you are back, Ted needs to see you. It's important, Daniel,' she insisted as she saw him about to object. 'I'm sure Lucas and his friend will excuse you for the few minutes it will take,' she maintained firmly.

Still flushed, Daniel produced a brittle laugh as he turned to his friend. 'Sorry, you know how it is. The place would fall apart without me! I'll see you later,' he promised before turning towards the shed.

Which left Megan facing Lucas and the woman. It was the blonde she turned to. 'I hope you'll forgive us for squabbling in front of you, but Terrell's has that effect on us, I'm afraid,' she apologised, only to receive a coolly distant smile for her pains.

'That's quite all right,' the blonde replied, sounding bored, and turned to smile up at Lucas. 'I'll wait by the car, darling. Don't be long. We have a date. . .remember?' With that pointed rejoinder, she cast another aloof smile at Megan, and left them.

Amused rather than put out, Megan stared after her. 'I'd be careful if I were you, Lucas. That pretty much sounded like she was staking a claim!' she drawled, turning back to him.

He was grinning, but there was something at the back of his eyes she couldn't identify. 'I'm always careful where women are concerned.'

Her brows lifted disarmingly. 'Mmm, I know. Safety in numbers, right?'

'Something like that,' he agreed easily, crossing his arms and taking his weight on one leg.

Of all the constants in the universe, Lucas was the one she was most sure of. 'You haven't changed, have you?'

'Unlike you. You look very sophisticated these days, Red. Very cool and in control.'

He was the only one who had ever called her that. It had irritated her as a teenager, but now she found that it sounded altogether different. Somehow darkly sweet and intimate. It sent a shiver along her spine, and she suddenly felt anything but cool.

'I work in a predominantly male field, so it wouldn't do my career any good to be seen as an emotional female,' she responded, hoping he wouldn't notice the inexplicable increase in her breathing.

Lucas's only evident reaction was to quirk one eyebrow. 'I'm surprised you're still here. I imagined you would have married long ago.'

Yes, he would think that, but a lot had happened since he had been away. He couldn't have known his comment would hurt, and that she would have to grit her teeth to laugh and make the statement she was now known for. 'What? Hand myself over to some man? You must be joking!' It was a glib answer, one polished to perfection by years of use. 'I decided years ago that marriage wasn't for me, and nothing has happened to change my mind,' she added for good measure. Glancing up at him, she discovered that for once she had surprised him.

'That doesn't sound like the Megan I remember. She waxed lyrical about making some man happy and raising a dozen kids. The last I heard you were crazy about Chris Baxter. What happened to him?'

Megan was shaken by the soft question. She had forgotten that Lucas had left before she'd broken up with Chris. She had hurt him, and her only excuse was that she had been too young to use finesse. Too overwhelmed by events to limit the damage. She knew better now. Years later she had apologised to Chris, and he had forgiven her, but they had never again been friends.

'We split up,' she shrugged, as if it had been no big deal. 'It didn't ruin his life. He's married now, with two small children,' she pointed out lightly.

'They could have been yours,' Lucas declared next, and Megan had to glance down quickly, pretending to remove an imaginary speck of dust from her blouse, before she had the necessary control to look him squarely in the eye.

'No, they couldn't. I'm not mother material. They'd disrupt my life, and I prefer it the way it is.' One day she might even believe it, she thought wryly.

Lucas frowned, shaking his head. 'So you're a career woman now?'

Megan smiled over-brightly. 'Absolutely. I've outgrown those childish fancies. I'm not looking for the right man, any more than you're looking for the right woman,' she retorted, feeling herself back on safe ground.

Now his smile grew. 'Who says I'm not looking? I just haven't found her yet.'

Megan looked sceptical. 'You mean you'd give up your lifestyle for just one woman?'

'Like that.' Lucas snapped his fingers. 'Its been a longer search than I expected.'

'And you've seen no reason not to enjoy yourself in the meantime,' she mocked, struggling with a strange emotion which appeared to be knotting her stomach. 'I thought you were looking a little jaded. Perhaps you ought to slow down. You're not getting any younger, you know, Lucas,' she advised sardonically.

'Wherever did you get this idea that I'm some kind of super-stud?' Lucas laughed, a full, rich sound which curled its way along her senses and set them fluttering.

Megan registered her reaction with a sharp intake of breath. Out of a clear blue sky she suddenly realised she wasn't responding to an old friend, but to a virile man who possessed physical magnetism in spades. She was a little surprised to find herself no more immune than the next woman. For as long as she could remember, Lucas had simply been just Lucas. Now her brain was having to do some rapid readjusting to the novel idea, whilst her senses were already several laps ahead!

'Probably from the way you change your women as often as you change your socks,' she drawled with oodles of irony, glad she had learned to hide her feelings because Lucas would have had a field-day with them.

'You've been reading too many papers, but I find it interesting that you bothered to read about me at all,' he remarked and she laughed this time.

'I've always been rather partial to horror stories,' she returned drily.

'Some day someone is going to give you a well-deserved beating,' Lucas growled, and Megan laughed again.

'You're not going to reserve that pleasure for yourself?'

'Believe me, I would, if it wasn't for the fact that Dan would probably tear me limb from limb.'

She grimaced, knowing that these days Daniel was more likely to lend him a hand! Nevertheless, she grinned. 'That's what brothers are for,' she quipped, and out of the corner of her eye caught sight of the blonde's angry scowl. 'Er...your friend seems a little put out,' she murmured, and Lucas glanced from the humour in her eyes to his companion.

'You're right. I'd better go and soothe her ruffled feathers.' He glanced at his watch. 'Tell Dan I'll be back as soon as I've booked into a hotel.'

Megan was surprised. She had assumed this was a flying visit. 'You're staying down here?'

His teeth flashed as he smiled. 'For a while. Think you can put up with me?'

'In small doses I even quite like you,' Megan admitted, then cocked her head to one side as she heard a bell ringing. 'That's the phone. I have to go, sorry,' she apologised, already on the move, and waved her hand in his general direction as she hurried towards the office.

Inside, Megan dashed for the desk, grabbing up the receiver to gasp a rushed, 'Hello.'

The voice which came down the line was familiar and disappointing, and she realised she had still been hoping to hear from that wretched German. 'Oh, Mark, it's you,' she replied, unwittingly ungracious, and turned to lean her weight against the edge of the desk whilst they talked.

However, as she did so, she faced the window, from where, framed in perfect view, she could see Lucas and the blonde were locked together in a passionate embrace. Standing beside the car, oblivious to who might be watching, the blonde seemed intent on eating him up alive, and Lucas didn't look as if he minded! Mere seconds later they parted with patent reluctance, and she watched as they held a short conversation before both climbed into the car and Lucas drove off.

Megan experienced a curious mixture of emotions. She really didn't care who he kissed, and yet seeing the blonde draped around him had made her feel furious with him. Which was totally ridiculous under the circumstances. Good Lord, this was Lucas. The playboy of Europe! The. . .

'Hello! Hello! Megan? Are you there?'

With a gasp of contrition, Megan belatedly realised she had left Mark dangling on the end of the line. 'Oh, good heavens! Yes, I'm here, Mark. Sorry, but I. . . er. . .got distracted,' she invented hastily. 'Did you want something?'

'Just to check if we're still on for tonight.'

'Of course. I'm looking forward to it,' she responded cheerfully, although it wasn't quite true. She had been dating Mark for a couple of months now, and though she liked him well enough she had the uneasy feeling that he might be one of her mistakes.

His chuckle was intimate. 'Good. I've chosen somewhere quiet and romantic, where we can be alone,' he claimed, and she stiffened, her thumbs pricking like mad. Oh, Lord, not again!

'Oh, um, that sounds wonderful,' she lied as her heart sank to her boots. Maybe she was wrong, but she really didn't think so. She'd just have to play it by ear. 'Where are we going?' she asked, and then spent an uncomfortable ten minutes having her worst fears realised, before Mark rang off, promising to pick her up at eight-thirty. It was not going to be a pleasant evening, but there was no avoiding it. Mark would have to go.

Feeling dispirited, she went to the washroom to freshen up. They were in the middle of a heatwave, and the humidity made her uncomfortably sticky. The cold water she splashed on her face felt wonderful.

Finally reaching for the towel, she stood back to look at herself critically in the mirror.

What she saw was a twenty-six-year-old woman, taller than average, with a generously curved body, right now clad in jade trousers and a white silk shirt. Her riot of rich auburn hair framed a heart-shaped face whose main feature, in her opinion, was a pair of slanted green eyes. She failed to see the charms of a slightly retroussé nose and a generous mouth, even though they created a total picture which had men beating a path to her door.

A brooding reflection clouded her eyes, and she reached for her brush, dragging it through her hair. Fate had a black sense of humour. Nature had fashioned her to attract a mate, had endowed her with every feminine instinct to achieve that purpose, and she had wanted nothing more, until fate had stepped in. Now, whilst she enjoyed dating, she wasn't looking for a husband. As her group of friends began to pair off, she remained determinedly single.

Most thought she had ice water in her veins, but they were mistaken. She had had an affair once, and it had been a disaster. She had been at university at the time, and feeling particularly alone. She had gone into it for all the wrong reasons, and they had both ended up being hurt. She had discovered that sexual satisfaction was no substitute for emotional involvement. And, since that was all she could offer, she had resolved never to go down that road again.

She had developed an instinct for knowing which men wanted more than she had to give, and avoided them. Occasionally she made mistakes, but she rectified them quickly, gaining for herself a reputation for coldness. She didn't mind. She would not offer more than she could give, nor take more than she deserved. It was the creed she had chosen to live by. And if, as sometimes happened, she was physically attracted to a man, she ignored it, burying herself in her work until the feeling passed.

Her career had become everything—her family and her life. She intended to make Terrell's a world-renowned name for quality and innovation. Her pride in her work was all the satisfaction she needed. A reaffirmation which brought a glitter to her eyes, and she turned away from her reflection, heading for the door.

Back in the office, she glanced to where her drawing-board stood to one end of the room. She resisted the urge to tinker with a new design, turning her back on it to round the desk and sink down onto the seat. There was more than enough paperwork to keep her busy for the rest of the day.

In the beginning Daniel had taken more than an equal interest in the running of the boatyard, but these days she very rarely saw him pick up a paper unless she forced him to. It wasn't that she minded the work, but she did mind the change in him. She couldn't explain it. When he'd first received his inheritance, he had had such enthusiasm, but these last few months he had acted as if he couldn't stand the place. He didn't seem to care about anything except going to the races with his fast friends.

She found herself increasingly angry with him, help-lessly so, because he refused to talk about it. The problem was, he wasn't a good judge of horses, and lost more money than they could afford. If he wasn't careful, they would lose the yard too. They must have a serious talk, and soon, if she could make him stand still long enough.

Not long afterwards, the object of her thoughts came through the door. Daniel dropped down heavily onto a vacant chair and rubbed a hand over his eyes. She refused to feel sorry for him, though the lines and unhealthy pallor on his face caused her concern. Unbidden, the memory of Lucas's lithe figure filled her mind. She didn't want to compare them, for that was unfair, yet there was no denying that Daniel was just a little bit less of everything than Lucas. Not as tall, not as muscular, and his handsomeness had a slightly weak quality to it.

Instantly she felt disloyal to have found Daniel wanting, but at the same time it served to remind her that loyalty was a rare commodity at the moment. Grimly, she crossed her arms, but when she spoke she simply sounded tired. 'How much did you lose this time, Daniel?'

Though it shouldn't have, her question appeared to take him unawares, rousing his anger. His temper had been on a short lead lately, too. 'No more than I could afford,' he snapped, then eyed the room irritably. 'Why are you always stuck in this tomb? It's turning you into a real bitch, Meg. I don't know how you stand it!'

She ignored the unflattering comment, knowing it to be a diversionary tactic. 'Just be thankful that I can. Somebody has to see that Terrell's runs smoothly, seeing as you've abdicated all involvement in favour of enjoying yourself with your so-called friends!' she retorted.

Daniel jumped up, ramming his hands into his jeans pockets. 'They are my friends!' he insisted angrily, and she sighed.

'No, they're not. They're just using you. Why can't you see that?' It was so clear to her. They would drop him as soon as the money ran out. Which might be all too terrifyingly close.

'Why can't you see that I'm not as stupid as you think? You're always complaining! You've never respected me, never thought I could know what I was doing!'

The accusation took her aback, and she caught her breath sharply. 'That's unfair! I did respect you.'

He didn't miss the qualification she had been unable to omit. 'Did?' he charged harshly.

It hurt her to admit it, but she wouldn't leave it unsaid if there was a chance that it could do some good. 'How can I respect you when you behave so foolishly? You just make me mad at you!'

'I had noticed,' Daniel said sourly. 'What exactly is it you don't approve of? My right to do what I like with my own money?'

Of course he had a point, but she would be failing in her duty if she didn't try to make him see sense. 'I just think—'

'I don't give a damn what you think,' he interrupted rudely, and colour rose in her cheeks as she lost her temper.

'I know. You don't care what anyone thinks, just so long as they don't stop you from enjoying yourself!' she declared disgustedly.

His fist thudded onto the desk. 'Its my life, for better or worse! What the hell business is it of yours how I live it?'

Megan shoved the chair back as she shot to her feet. 'It's my business because you're my brother, Daniel, and I care what happens to you. Beyond that, this is my livelihood too. I have to see the results of what you're doing and it sickens me!' she returned, alarmed at the violence of the argument, for it was so unlike Daniel to raise his voice.

His face was mottled and angry. 'You get well paid for any inconvenience!'

She paled, cut to the quick. 'Dear God, Daniel, how dare you say that to me? I work damn hard to keep this business going, without any help from you.' Without pay, either. She'd been robbing Peter to pay Paul for months, and there was none left over to pay Megan! She was living off her own dwindling assets, which he would have found out if he had had the interest to do the accounts. She hadn't told him yet, but the day was fast approaching when she would have to.

His head went back at her accusation. 'Believe me, I'm truly grateful,' he said ungraciously, and her lips parted on a sharp intake of breath.

'You know, Daniel, this business won't be able to support your lifestyle for ever. You can't keep gambling with your future this way.' And mine, she added silently. 'You're pushing everything to the edge. What happens when you go over it?'

If she'd thought that would reach him, she was wrong. 'Then you can say "I told you so",' he sneered, and turned accusing eyes on her. 'What did you do with Lucas—scare him off too?'

She smothered an urge to snap back. 'No, he had to go. He said to tell you he would be back later.'

'Lucas was always more than a match for you, wasn't he?' Daniel taunted nastily. 'Well, as I'm not supposed to be here, I'm going back to the house,' he declared challengingly, and shouldered a surprised Ted aside as the man unfortunately attempted to enter the room at the same time as he was leaving it.

Megan sank down on her chair, finding she was shaking. They'd never argued like that before, never, and she wasn't afraid to admit that it had alarmed her. Daniel had always been a gentle soul. Weak, yes, but gentle. For him to act so out of character meant something was badly wrong.

Ted turned from watching Daniel's exit to study her. 'What was that all about?'

Megan sighed heavily, raising her hands in a gesture of futility. 'I can't even talk to him any more. He just doesn't listen.'

Ted humphed. 'That crowd he hangs around with are no good,' he pronounced gently.

'I know. He didn't used to be like this. I'm hoping

that if only we can get him away from those ghouls
he'll change.'

'Maybe. I'll make no bones about it—Daniel's too
easily led. You do your best, love, but you're still only
his sister. He needs to face someone with a bit of fight
in them. Someone he'll respect, and who won't let him
take the easy route,' Ted stated firmly, and Megan
nodded.

'Unfortunately, people like that don't grow on trees.'
She grimaced despondently, and Ted scratched his
head wryly.

'No, but they own telephones,' he chuckled, making
Megan frown.

'OK, I'll fall for it. What do you mean?' she asked
drily.

Ted shook his head at her, despairing of her intelli-
gence. 'I mean Lucas, of course. Daniel told me who
the visitor was, and it occurred to me that he was
always good with your brother. Daniel always looked
up to him. Why don't you get Lucas to talk to him?'
He let the thought sink in.

Megan's eyes widened. He was right. She had said it
herself only a short while ago. But... 'How can I?
Daniel would never forgive me if I told Lucas all about
him.' She sighed, hating to see such a good idea go
west.

'Daniel's anger won't last, but once Terrell's is gone
it's gone for good!' Ted said gruffly, his hand on her
shoulder tempering the blow. 'Think on it. Meanwhile,
here's a list of supplies. I was ordered to give it to you.'

Megan couldn't help laughing as she took the paper.
'Surprise, surprise.'

'So, where is the man? I didn't see a car outside. Has
he gone?'

'Only to a hotel. He drove off with his playmate
some time ago,' she returned drily, and Ted shot
her a look.

'Playmate?'

Megan's lips curved in amusement. 'The ubiquitous blonde. Like that charge card, you'll never see him without one!'

'Aye, he was always one for the ladies, was Lucas,' he replied with a laugh as he left again.

Megan propped her chin on her hand. Ted had never spoken a truer word, especially about Lucas's influence over her brother. Or, to be more accurate, her half-brother. They had had the same father but different mothers. And thereby hung a tale. The situation had given Daniel a birthright to waste, and herself an inheritance so cruel, there was no room for tears.

She pushed the knowledge back into the recesses of her mind, refusing to think about it. However, she would give Ted's suggestion some thought. When you'd gone through every other means available without success, you were willing to consider anything.

In the meantime, work beckoned. With a sigh, she picked up her pen again, reaching for the nearest ledger, and for the second time that day was halted by the sound of a car. She recognised it this time, though, and went to the door. Lucas was just climbing out.

'Back so soon?' she asked sweetly, and Lucas grinned, making himself comfortable by resting his arms on the car roof.

'I didn't want to miss a minute of your sparkling company, Red.'

'It's just as well I know better than to believe you,' she responded drily. 'If you're looking for Daniel, he isn't here.'

Brows raised, Lucas glanced at his watch. 'Short day?'

Megan crossed her arms and leant against the door-frame. 'Every now and then he gives himself time off for good behaviour. You'll find him up at the house.'

Hopefully sleeping, and not drinking, she added silently.

'Thanks,' Lucas said, preparing to get back in the car. 'Why don't you join us?'

She could just imagine what Daniel would have to say to that! 'You know what they say—two's company, three's a crowd. You'll be able to talk more freely without me there. You must have lots to catch up on,' she refused politely.

'Don't you want to hear what I've been doing?' he taunted.

'Oh, I think I've got a pretty good idea!' she exclaimed sardonically, and he laughed.

'You're wrong, you know, but, if it pleases you to believe what you read, so be it,' Lucas declared, and with another of his blinding smiles, which left Megan rooted to the spot, he climbed into the car, started the engine and drove off.

She shuddered, scorched by a heat far stronger than the sun. When it came to dangerous weapons, Lucas's smile should be registered as lethal! Turning back into the office, she knew she would have the devil's own job trying to concentrate on anything as mundane as work. Reaching her desk, she picked up an invoice, resolutely ignoring the memory of eyes and a smile which seemed to be having the strangest effect on her.

CHAPTER TWO

IT WAS close to midnight when Mark brought his car to a halt outside the house, converted from two cottages, which Megan had shared with Daniel since their father died. It was a hot summer night, and the lounge windows were still thrown wide, muted light shining through them. Megan wished she were inside, not sitting in the sporty convertible, waiting for trouble.

The date had rung warning bells from the start, for not only had Mark chosen a secluded restaurant but he had presented her with flowers too. Her misgivings of earlier had been slowly consolidated, taking her appetite away. Although he didn't say so, she knew Mark took their relationship more seriously than she had thought, and this was his bid to take it a step further. Now, when he took her in his arms to kiss her goodnight, it was with a depth of passion he hadn't shown before. She didn't resist, but she didn't respond either, and when that fact finally got through he eased away to frown at her.

'Megan? Is something wrong?' he asked, puzzled, and Megan closed her eyes momentarily, bracing herself.

'Yes, Mark, I think there is,' she began gently but firmly. 'I like you very much, but . . .' She hesitated, reluctant to cause hurt. It shouldn't have come to this. Usually she read the signs, and could put an end to the association before there was any danger of misunderstanding. But she had been so preoccupied lately, she had totally misread the situation.

Beside her, Mark had tensed. 'But?' he queried

shortly, and she knew that tact was going to get her nowhere. She would have to be blunt.

'I don't want an affair.'

In the reflected light, she saw Mark smile and her heart sank. 'I know that, honey. I don't want an affair either.' He reached out, fingering a stray lock of her hair. 'Oh, Megan. I think I'm falling in love with you,' he declared huskily, and ice settled in her stomach.

Licking dry lips, she tried to be gentle. 'Don't fall in love with me, Mark. You'll be wasting your time.'

'Let me be the judge of that,' he countered huskily, clearly thinking she was playing hard to get, and Megan knew that subtlety simply would not work.

Turning in her seat so that her hair pulled free and his hand fell away, she eyed him squarely. 'Listen to me. I'm sorry, but I don't love you, Mark. I won't ever love you. I like you a lot, and enjoy your company, but I'm not looking for more than that. I'd like to continue seeing you, but only if you can accept my rules.'

He heard her out in silence, and she could feel him withdrawing from her. 'And if I can't accept them?'

Megan felt her heart sink further, for she knew this was going to be one of the bad times, but her expression remained firm. 'Then this is goodbye.'

She could feel his anger surging towards her, and something nasty flickered in his eyes. 'You know, I didn't believe it. They tried to warn me, but I argued them down. Now I see you really are the heartless bitch they said you were, aren't you?'

She had heard worse, but she flinched anyway. So much for love. Gathering up her bag and her poise, she sent him a cool smile. 'I'll take that as no, then, shall I?' Climbing out, she shut the door with care. 'Goodbye, Mark. I'm sorry it had to end this way.'

He gunned the engine before delivering a parting shot, and she had to strain to hear what he said over the noisy revving. 'My mistake. I thought you were simply wary of involvement, but now I see you don't have anything to give a man. I pity you, but I figure I'm well out of it!'

Even though she had expected it, Megan still caught her breath as she stared after the departing tail-lights, feeling weary to her bones. His words hurt and tears stung the backs of her eyes, but she blinked them away because she was never going to feel guilty again for allowing someone to believe things which were not true. However, such confrontations always left her that little bit more diminished, so it was as well they didn't come along too often.

With a sigh, she turned to go inside, and it was then that she saw the shadow outlined in the lounge window. It moved as she did, and she frowned as she walked indoors, not liking the idea of having been overheard, and yet grateful that Daniel was at least home before her for once. Tossing her bag onto the hall table, she entered the room on her left.

Stretching and running her fingers through her hair, she kicked off her shoes. 'This is a nice surprise, Da. . .' She got no further, because at that point she discovered that the man in the room wasn't her brother at all, but Lucas. Her lips parted in shock and her rounded eyes darted to the window, as if to confirm what she already knew.

Now standing by the fireplace, with his arm resting on the mantel, Lucas observed her in amusement. 'I found it very edifying,' he remarked, confirming her suspicions. 'Do you always discard importunate suitors so delicately?'

Pale with shock, Megan realised her hands were still raised, and hastily lowered them to her sides, using the precious seconds to recover. It had been bad enough imagining Daniel hearing what had transpired. To discover that it was Lucas was unsettling. Not that she cared what he thought. Her reasons were as valid as ever, and she would not explain, even if she could have.

So she shrugged, pretending an insouciance she was far from feeling right then. 'Only those who won't take no for an answer,' she said blithely, flinging herself gracefully into the corner of the couch and crossing her legs with a slither of silk.

Lucas's eyes followed her down, lingering to caress the shapely curves of her calves with an intensity which brought a tiny gasp to her lips. Megan felt a tingle of warmth ignite in the pit of her stomach. Her eyes widened. She couldn't recall the last time she had experienced such an instantaneous kick of desire, but it wasn't so long that she had forgotten what it felt like. The surprise came in feeling it now, with Lucas. Unbidden, a tingle of anticipation sent a delicate shiver over her skin.

'Determined to keep all men at arm's length, Red?' Lucas's mocking query pierced her bemusement, and with a swift mental shake for allowing herself to be so easily distracted Megan manufactured an equally mocking smile.

'I'm a modern woman. I reserve the right to choose who I want to have affairs with,' she responded lightly, though in truth her 'affairs' were in the singular. Which could hardly have been said of the man who stood before her.

As she spoke, one part of her brain noted that the elegant dinner suit he wore could not hide the sheer power of the man. She had always known he was handsome, but she had registered his physical magnetism clinically, not receptive to the signals he sent out. She was tuned into them now, though, with a vengeance, and it made the hairs stand up on her skin.

'Making sure you only choose those men you can control, no doubt,' Lucas remarked coolly. 'What are you afraid of?'

Thick lashes dropped to veil her expression from him. 'Afraid' was such a timid word, meant for fanciful things. Her terrors had substance, but she had the power to control them—an awesome power that she could never, ever abdicate, for it was, quite simply, a matter of life and death.

That brought a grim smile to her lips as she looked up, taking his question as it was meant—at face value. 'What are *you* afraid of? You're conspicuously unattached yourself. You must have your own rules about how close any woman is allowed to get.'

He acknowledged that with an inclination of his head. 'True, but my method of parting is less Draconian. That poor fool outside bared his soul to you, and you ground it in the dirt. Where's your compassion?'

She stared at his austere face without flinching. He was making a value judgement, and she couldn't blame him, based on what he had heard. She had sounded heartless, but to tell him she had only been cruel to be kind would lead to demands for explanations, and she had decided long ago that she would apologise for nothing. In a harsh world, only the strong survived. And she *would* be strong. There was no other course for her.

'He didn't love me,' she said evenly. 'And even if he did he won't tomorrow.'

Across from her, Lucas shook his head incredulously. 'How did you get to be so hard?' he asked, and she almost laughed.

With years of practice and determination she had built a shell as hard as nails, but underneath... Tonight's episode was evidence enough that she was still vulnerable. Sometimes she wondered if there would be anything worthwhile left inside when the wall became complete. Would it be an empty shell of a life? How ironic. How . . .

But she would not think of that. Not now. Not ever.

'Where's Daniel?' she asked, ignoring the question and thereby sealing his opinion of her. She told herself she didn't care.

After the briefest of pauses, Lucas accepted the change of subject with a twist of his lips. 'I haven't the faintest idea.'

That had her sitting up straighter. 'What do you mean?' Surely if they had gone out together he would know where her brother was?

'I mean I have no idea where he spent the evening. I was otherwise engaged,' he informed her, and Megan was on her feet in an instant.

'But. . .if you weren't with Daniel, what are you doing here?' she asked, anxiety making the question sharper than she intended.

Lucas hesitated, frowning himself as something occurred to him. 'Dan didn't tell you, did he?'

All sorts of dire possibilities as to what she didn't know danced across her mind, and she clamped her arms about her waist, bracing herself for trouble. 'You may as well tell me the worst,' she invited in a flat tone, which brought his blue gaze to lock questioningly with hers.

'You sound as if the world might have come to an end,' he said with the faintest hint of a laugh.

She didn't smile. If Daniel had gone off to another race meeting, it might very well be the end. 'I'm too tired for games, Lucas. Just get it over with, will you?' she snapped, then sighed heavily. It was no use blaming him for Daniel's shortcomings. She waved a dismissive hand. 'I'm sorry. I . . .' The rest tailed off helplessly, and Lucas took pity on her.

'When I met Dan this afternoon, he invited me to stay here,' he explained concisely, and Megan blinked at him stupidly.

'That's it? I thought . . .' She took a steadying breath, and produced a rather tired smile. Never mind what she had thought, she had been mistaken, and the relief was heady. 'I ought to know Daniel would do something like that without consulting me!' she exclaimed wryly, and Lucas frowned.

'You have some problem with me staying here?'

Only in so far as it gave her another mouth to feed and another body to clean up after. They had dispensed with the housekeeper months ago, and not unnaturally everything fell onto her broad shoulders. By not telling her, Daniel had probably been paying her back for what she had said earlier. If he expected her to complain, he was mistaken.

'Not at all. You're very welcome to stay, Lucas, though you'll have to give me a moment to make up the spare bed.'

'There's no need. I'm quite capable of making my own bed, if you'll show me where the sheets are kept,' he countered, walking towards her, and as he did so Megan caught sight of a smudge of pink by his mouth. It was the same colour the blonde had worn earlier, and she realised with whom he had been 'otherwise engaged'.

It was automatic to reach up and rub the revealing smudge away with her thumb. 'How careless of you to leave the evidence showing. There, that's better. That shade of pink does nothing for you, you know,' she taunted silkily, and would have moved away, only she suddenly found her wrist caught in a loose but unbreakable grip.

Lucas's blue eyes glinted wickedly. 'Perhaps I left it for you to find, Red,' he said softly, and though her heart gave a wild lurch she quirked her eyebrows tauntingly.

'Now why would you want to do that?' she countered, hoping he didn't hear that touch of breathlessness in her voice.

His smile was slow and seductive. 'Why, to see what

you would do, of course. A person's reaction can be very revealing.'

Her stomach did a reverse flip before settling again. 'And what did mine reveal?' she challenged, tinglingly aware of the heat of his touch and the warmth of his closeness. She was all at once very wide awake, with all senses functioning.

'That you think I'm as shallow, if not shallower, than the women I take out.'

Megan grinned and tipped her head to one side. 'I did notice you had found another blonde clone,' she remarked by way of confirmation.

Lucas's eyes glittered as he raised an eyebrow questioningly. 'Blonde clone?'

Finding the exchange wildly exhilarating, she looked right back at him. 'My, you must be in a bad way if you haven't noticed they all look alike. They even have the same names, like Sophie, Stephanie or Sylvia,' she remarked, and his lips twitched as he released her wrist.

'I had no idea you'd made such a close study of the situation.'

Megan sighed elaborately, hiding the fact that her flesh still felt the imprint of his. She favoured him with an old-fashioned look. 'It's hard not to when your picture, plus "friend", is plastered across the newspapers almost daily. By the way, I hope you fed what's-her-name tonight, thus sparing us from watching her try to make a meal out of you in public!'

'You saw that, did you? Watching is never as much fun as participation. A very. . .affectionate woman, Sonja.'

'Ah, Sonja!' Megan exclaimed sardonically. 'How very. . .Nordic.'

A devilish gleam entered his eyes. 'Only by name. By nature she's pure Latin. Didn't you enjoy the show?'

Now that he mentioned it, no, she hadn't. 'It made

me think of the tigers in the zoo at feeding time, when they pounce on their food and tear it apart with their teeth!' she declared, with a delicate shudder of distaste.

Lucas's lips curved appreciatively at the analogy. 'You think I should fear for my life?'

Her eyes danced. 'I'd say you should fear more for your freedom.'

He pretended to consider that. 'You think she intends to have me?' he asked, and Megan laughed.

'Have you? She already thinks she's got you! If I were you, I'd be feeling very nervous right now. If you listen hard enough, I'm certain you'll be able to hear church bells ringing!' she enlarged with a liberal amount of unholy enjoyment.

Lucas grinned, and the gleam in his eyes deepened. 'You'd really enjoy seeing me caught, wouldn't you, Red?'

She grinned right back at him. 'I find the idea quite poignant. The biter bit, so to speak.'

His teeth flashed whitely as his smile broadened. 'It's a wonder you haven't thought of having a go yourself.'

'I may be stupid sometimes, but I'm not insane!' she riposted neatly, though her heart actually started to race at the very idea.

'I'm surprised you didn't say desperate,' he commented drily.

'I was trying to be polite,' she lied brazenly, and Lucas threw back his head and laughed, causing her to watch him in fascination.

After a moment or two he recovered his poise and observed her with his head tilted to one side. 'You know, Red, I'm glad you haven't changed too much. You're still as fiery as your hair. It would have been a shame to see all that vibrancy subdued. You're much more entertaining this way.'

Megan rounded her eyes at him. 'More entertaining than Sonja?' she probed.

'Within reason. Sonja's talents are more. . .womanly,' Lucas said softly, and his remark was all the more deadly for it.

The enjoyment died out of her so swiftly that it was quite shocking. She simply hadn't been expecting the cloaked attack, had allowed the novelty of her awareness of him to make her drop her guard. With a faint laugh she glanced down at her hands, was surprised to find that they carried a fine tremor, and dug deep for her composure before she looked up again, smiling with icy humour.

'You think Mark's right, don't you? That I'm missing something quintessentially feminine.'

Lucas shrugged. 'Most men would prefer more warmth and less frostbite,' he conceded and Megan unexpectedly saw red.

'It's amazing!' she exclaimed angrily. 'If I appeared to promise something and then didn't deliver, you'd call me a tease. Because I chose to say no, you call me cold.'

Lucas studied her fierce expression with interest. 'Oh, I wouldn't say cold exactly. More cold-blooded. You have to be in control, and no quarter is given to anyone who oversteps the mark.'

Baldly put, but true. She wasn't prepared to compromise on that part of her life. If you avoid involvement, you can't cause pain—a maxim she kept to herself.

'There is no point in having rules if you don't obey them,' she insisted, and drew a frown from him.

'How can there be rules in love? You never know when it's going to strike,' he countered, and she smiled, seeing the opening.

'Precisely my point. I don't want love to strike, and my rules are there to make sure it doesn't. There's no room for love in my life. Love means marriage and a family. I don't want children. I'm not the maternal sort. And I certainly don't want to be tied to one man for life. Love is a trap, and I want to be free to do anything I please with my life.' There were so many lies in there, she ought to have had her fingers crossed, but Lucas didn't know that.

He took her at her word. 'Interesting. There's just one thing you've forgotten. Life has a way of scuttling the best laid plans.'

She knew that only too painfully well, which was why she left nothing to chance. 'Not mine. I have no intention of being taken by surprise. My life is exactly the way I want it,' she said with the utmost conviction, sounding as cold-blooded as he had accused her of being. Raising her chin defiantly, she met his look and damned him to criticise her.

'I take back what I said—you certainly have changed, Red,' Lucas uttered with a shake of his head.

And not for the better, obviously. She had expected his condemnation, but not the hurt it brought with it. She had thought she was beyond that, but apparently not. She shrugged it off with an unrepentant laugh. 'Oh, dear, I appear to have shocked you!' she exclaimed, pretending an amusement she was far from feeling.

Lucas didn't laugh this time. If she'd been asked to describe his expression, she would have said it was regretful. 'I'm trying to equate the warm, lovely girl I used to know with the woman standing before me now.'

Megan found she had to turn away to swallow the lump of emotion which blocked her throat. Walking to the window, she reached out to pull it shut. 'Did you expect me to stay a child for ever?' she asked as she drew the curtains and faced him again.

He was watching her as if she was a particularly tricky puzzle he was determined to crack. 'No, but to go to such extremes is unusual. What happened to you, Red?'

How strange. Nobody else had ever asked that. They had simply accepted everything she said and did. It upset her to find Lucas so perceptive, but it was too late for confidences. So she frowned as if she didn't understand. 'Nothing happened. I just grew up.' And made some decisions about her life which had been painful but unavoidable, she thought.

Artfully she stifled a yawn. 'It's getting late. If you come with me, I'll get the sheet and duvet. You don't mind using a duvet, I hope? I know that some men simply can't abide them.' She was babbling, but she didn't care. She had had just about all she could safely take of the conversation.

'The duvet will be fine,' Lucas confirmed, watching her carefully, so that she felt rather like a specimen under a microscope. He indicated that she should go before him, and she did so with relief.

Leading the way upstairs, she went to the laundry cupboard on the landing and handed him the sweet-smelling covers.

'Are you sure you can manage?' she asked politely, and Lucas nodded.

'I'll be fine. Goodnight, Megan,' he said sombrely, and headed down the corridor towards the spare room.

'Goodnight, Lucas. Sleep well,' she called after him but if he heard he made no sign. Biting her lip, she went downstairs again to secure the house, leaving only one light glowing in the hall before collecting her things and going up to her room.

Once inside, she threw the window wide and sank down onto the window-seat. All things considered, this had to be one of the worst evenings of her life. First Mark, then Lucas. Separately the confrontations would have been bad enough, but back to back... She felt exhausted. No matter how convinced she was of the rightness of her actions, defending them always left her feeling drained. Tonight had been especially wearing, for, although Mark only knew her as an adult woman, Lucas had a lifetime of memories to compare her with.

It was funny how neither her father nor Daniel had remarked on the woman she had become by the time she'd returned from university. Only Lucas had found the change out of character. She found that she didn't like him thinking less of her, but there was no way to alter that. Not without revealing too much. She had her pride. She did not want pity. She refused to feel sorry for herself, and would abhor having anyone feeling sorry for her. That was an inherent part of her rules.

She had been eighteen years old when she'd made them. One day she had been looking forward to university, followed by love, marriage and a family. The next, everything had changed. That year her mother had developed cancer, and, as so often happened, within months they had lost her. Megan had barely got over the shock of it when another had followed in the form of a letter. What Kate Terrell had never been able to tell her daughter during her life had been revealed to her in the scrawled lines she'd read in the solicitor's musty office.

A stunned Megan had learned that Kate Terrell had had a genetic disease. It was hereditary, and there was no cure. Passed down through the female line, it was not life-threatening to Megan or any daughter she might have, but it would be fatal to a son. Boys rarely survived infancy.

Curling her feet under her, Megan folded her arms about her waist, arming herself against the memory. She hadn't wanted to believe it, but when she had gone away to university she had consulted a doctor, and that was when the nightmare had begun. She had had tests, and they had confirmed her mother's story. She had the gene and would pass it on to her children. Too stunned to react then, in the following months she had gone through every emotion possible between anger and despair. Hating her mother for not telling her. Hating the world for being so unfair.

Megan rested her head back against the panelling and closed her eyes. She remembered the doctor insisting that she could go ahead and lead a normal life—it had made her want to laugh and cry. For how could she ever have a normal life? To her that meant a husband and family. Children. Knowing what she knew, how could she have them? How could she condemn a daughter to go through what she was going through? How could she carry a son under her heart for nine months, and then slowly watch him die?

Peace had only come with the acceptance that there was nothing she could do about herself, and carrying on the way she was would only make her ill. The past was unchanging, but she could do something about the future. She had seen very clearly what she must do. She would not gamble with her unborn children. She would end the misery here, by making sure she was the last of her line. It was a choice only she could make. She wasn't a martyr. She hadn't enjoyed the pain of her decision, but she'd known it was the right one, and it had given her the peace she'd sought.

That it also meant she would never marry was something she'd accepted unflinchingly. If she couldn't have it all, she would rather have nothing. No regrets, no recriminations, her commitment would be to her career. She had lived by her decision, and only once had she given in to her loneliness, her need for closeness, and had an affair.

Toby had loved her but she hadn't loved him. He had thought he could change that, and for a while she had let him try. But she had always known there was no future for them, and that by allowing him to think otherwise she wasn't being fair. The pain and guilt had been hard to live with, even after she had ended the affair. She had made it a rule after that never to get involved with anyone.

Sighing heavily, she combed her fingers through her hair. Lord, she hated hurting anyone, but she couldn't take without giving, and because she couldn't give she wouldn't allow herself to take. So she kept everyone at bay because it was safer that way. Sometimes things went wrong, like tonight, and sometimes she met the unexpected. Like this attraction she was feeling towards Lucas. . . It was certainly startling, but she had been attracted to men before and nothing had come of it. This would turn out to be the same, she was sure. So she would ignore it, and when Lucas left, whenever that might be, things would be back to how they were.

Bolstered by that sound piece of common sense, Megan stretched her weary bones and finally prepared for bed.

The next day dawned bright and sunny and, refreshed, Megan donned a white vest-top and pleated khaki shorts which showed off an expanse of tanned flesh gathered from hours of messing about on the water. As she slipped her feet into a pair of trainers, she hoped she might find time for some sailing this afternoon, though she wouldn't hold her breath.

On her way down to the kitchen she looked in Daniel's room, and wasn't surprised to find the bed undisturbed. Telling herself she wouldn't read more into it than she had to, she skipped down the stairs, sniffing the air. The scent of coffee perking wafted up to her. Frowning, because it was still early, she pushed open the kitchen door to find Lucas seated at the table sipping at a steaming mug.

He glanced up as she halted in surprise, his eyes running appreciatively down her slim figure to her long, tanned legs. A smile curved his lips.

'Very nice,' he complimented softly, and Megan felt

a resurgence of that tingling awareness skitter over her nerves.

'You don't look so bad yourself,' she responded, which was an understatement, because in rather disreputably faded jeans and a body-hugging black T-shirt he was a sight to please a woman's sore eyes. And her eyes, she realised wryly, must have been very sore, because the day had suddenly and unexpectedly taken on an extra sparkle. She crossed to the refrigerator with her pulse just a little heightened. She was beginning to see why those women ignored the danger signs. There was something about Lucas which could make you not give a damn.

'Have you had breakfast?' The prosaic question settled her pulse back to normal.

Lucas twisted in his seat to follow her with his eyes. 'I was going to, then I recalled you had a tartar in charge of the kitchen and thought better of it,' he explained, watching her remove eggs, bacon, butter and milk.

Megan tutted and reached down a saucepan. 'Bella was a very nice woman. Unfortunately she's no longer with us, but I can assure you this housekeeper is not the jealous type, and will cook you scrambled eggs and bacon if you're interested,' she said, facing him again.

She didn't know whether to be flattered or not by his surprise. 'You?'

'I do know how to cook, so you can be sure I won't poison you accidentally,' she warned, tongue-in-cheek. 'So, eggs and bacon?'

Humour-lines crinkled up by his eyes at her allusion. 'They're fine by me,' he agreed instantly, and watched how effortlessly she went about the task. 'Is there anything I can do to help?'

She sent him a doubtful look over her shoulder. 'If I can trust you not to burn it, you can make some toast.

Bread is in the bin and the toaster is over there.' She nodded to her left.

For the next few minutes the scene was quite domestic as they worked together in perfect harmony. Megan's heart gave a curious little jerk as she recognised the fact, then she told herself sternly not to start reading anything into it. They had always got on when they weren't fighting. Which meant a fight was probably waiting just around the corner.

'What happened to your housekeeper?' They were sitting down eating the food they had prepared when Lucas returned to the subject.

Pausing with a forkful of fluffy egg halfway to her mouth, Megan shrugged. 'We decided we didn't really need her. Daniel is hardly ever here for meals, and the house isn't so big that I can't cope with the cleaning,' she lied, and felt him staring at her lowered head as she concentrated on her food.

'Why pay for something you can do yourself, right?' he remarked lightly, making her look at him suspiciously, wondering if he had guessed the truth.

But from his blandness, he apparently hadn't, and she relaxed. 'Absolutely,' she agreed, remembering how the economy had helped for a while.

'It's fortunate you're a good cook.'

It would have been all the same if she weren't! 'Perhaps scrambled eggs and bacon is all I'm good at,' she countered.

'Oh, I'm sure not,' Lucas argued with a nuance she had no trouble interpreting, and her heart missed a beat.

'If that's a sample of your much vaunted technique, I'm surprised it gets you anywhere!' she mocked, but he only grinned.

'There are a lot of women who would disagree with you about that.'

She sent him a pitying look. 'Heaven only knows

what those poor deluded women see in you,' she despaired, and began collecting up the dirty crockery.

Lucas held out his plate, but when she took it he refused to let it go. As she was bending over the table, the manoeuvre brought his head mere inches away from hers. 'You'd have to kiss me to find out,' he said invitingly, and, despite herself, her heart kicked against her breast as if trying to escape. She looked at his mouth and her stomach lurched. Lord, but he was potent, she thought, and managed to keep her composure by a monumental effort.

'I'll pass, thanks,' she replied, wincing inwardly at how husky her voice sounded, then almost forgot to breathe when she saw his eyes drop to her mouth.

'You're sure? I wouldn't mind obliging,' he added persuasively, and a tingling sensation passed over her lips, as if he had actually touched them.

Releasing the plate, Megan straightened up. 'Since you're in such an obliging mood, you can oblige me by doing the washing-up. Hot water is in the tap, detergent is on the drainer, and you'll find rubber gloves under the sink if you want to protect your lily-white hands!' she taunted, heading for the door with a wide grin on her face.

There was a bounce in her step as she grabbed up her bag and car keys, and she realised that she had almost forgotten how to really laugh. She had always enjoyed sparring with Lucas, and having got the better of him just now added an extra zest to the day.

She was humming as she drove her ancient Fiat into the yard, and Ted's lugubrious face twisted into a grin when she joined him in the shed moments later.

'You seem perky.'

Megan grinned. 'I left Lucas doing the washing-up,' she explained.

'Got him on a string already, have you?' Ted chortled. 'I guess we can expect fireworks to light up the place again.'

She didn't say anything, just smiled. Things had changed with Lucas's arrival, and perhaps Ted was right and he would bring them luck. Time would tell.

She saw very little of Lucas and Daniel over the next few days. They went out early and came back late, and she hoped good things would come from the time they spent together. She would have been happier if they'd gone out in the evenings too, but there they went their separate ways. She had no doubt what Daniel was doing—nor Lucas for that matter. No doubt the sexy Sonja was keeping him busy! Not that it bothered her. He could do what he liked, and it allowed her to get a grip on the fledgling attraction she had succumbed to.

A week slipped by without incident. Megan began work on a new design. As she sat at her drawing-board, her eyes traced the sleek lines. The craft would cut through the water so perfectly that Megan knew she could sell it if only they had the funds to build it and show it. She frowned. If she just altered this. . .

She didn't hear the footsteps approaching, and it was only when a shadow blocked out her light that she looked up to find Daniel beside her. Her smile faded as she took stock of his morning-after appearance. His clothes were clean: it was his face which looked wrinkled. Aware that he rarely sought her out unless he wanted something, she tossed down her pencil.

'You've come to the wrong place, haven't you? This is a boatyard,' she greeted him sardonically.

'I know what it is,' Daniel answered testily, transferring his gaze from her to the paper. 'Mmm, not bad.'

Megan brushed her hair back, her eyebrows rising at his grudging praise. 'Yes, well, I try to keep my hand in just in case a miracle happens,' she responded mockingly. 'What can I do for you? Or are you here to work?'

His eyes clashed with hers then darted away again. 'I need the key to the safe.'

Megan froze. The only things inside were the medals her great-grandfather had won in the First World War and her mother's jewellery. He knew that as well as she did. 'They belong to me, Daniel,' she reminded him.

Daniel's jaw clenched mutinously. 'You'll get them back, I swear! I only want to pawn them.'

She turned back to the drawing and began to re-trace a perfectly good line. 'No! You know if I let you take anything I'll never see it again.'

'I give you my word you will, Meg,' he swore, with a nervy edge to his voice which brought a tight smile to her lips.

'I'm sorry, Daniel, but your word isn't worth much these days,' she told him as she swung round to face him again.

Daniel dragged a hand through his hair. 'Thanks for the vote of confidence!' he snarled, and met her unflinching look. He swore silently. 'What happened to loyalty, Meg?'

'I expect you bet it on a horse that's still running! I don't understand you any more. You were going to have the best boatyard in the country. How can you let it all slip away?' she asked bluntly, hoping for an honest answer, but he merely looked stubborn.

'I work to live, not live to work!'

It was remarks such as those which made her so angry with him. All the anger and disappointment of the last months spilt over in an angry tirade. 'How dare you say that so glibly? What about our last two workers who put their faith in you? What do I tell them when I lay them off?'

Daniel didn't care for her tone. 'It won't come to that,' he protested, catching her arm.

'It already has, or are you too blind or too stupid to see?' she challenged, shaking him off.

Daniel flushed. 'Lay off me, Megan!' he growled harshly, grabbing up her mug of pencils and throwing it at the wall. 'Just lay off me, all right?' he ordered, and in a manner she was fast coming used to, he stormed out.

Megan found she was shaking. Daniel's actions had actually alarmed her to that extent, and she suddenly realised there was more to this than she'd thought. She didn't know what, but the icy lump in her stomach was warning enough. Her heart lurched. Oh, Daniel, what on earth have you got yourself into? she cried silently.

CHAPTER THREE

'PROBLEMS?' Lucas's lazy drawl came from behind her, and she spun round to find him in the doorway, his shoulder propped comfortably against the frame.

Taking a deep breath, she crossed the room to clear up the mess Daniel had made. 'Go away, Lucas!' she snapped, wondering how long he had been there and how much he had heard. Finishing the task, she set the sadly dented cup back in its usual place.

'Do you often fight?' he asked, and Megan winced at the realisation that he had witnessed that much at least.

'Don't you have anything to do besides poke your nose into other people's business?' she retorted, abandoning her drawing and going to the desk. Her hands were still trembling too much to draw a straight line, even with a ruler.

'Not right now,' Lucas replied smoothly.

Picking up a pile of folders, Megan carried them to the nearby filing cabinet, set them down on the top and proceeded to file them.

'You have the hide of a rhinoceros! What you saw was just a difference of opinion. We have them all the time,' she lied, watching him move away from the door to study her design.

'In that case I suggest you buy unbreakable furnishings or you'll have lost everything in a week!' he drawled back, without taking his eyes from the board. 'She's going to be beautiful,' he praised, tracing a line with his finger.

Megan smiled wryly, warmed by the unsolicited comment. 'Thanks. Now all I need is someone to commission me to build her.'

Lucas glanced up curiously. 'That shouldn't be a problem, surely? Dan said you were doing well.'

She heard the unspoken query and her lips twisted. 'He was ever an optimist. There's a recession on, you know.'

'I had heard something about it,' Lucas agreed as he wandered over to the desk. He ran a cursory eye over the ledgers she had spread out there. 'Since when have you been in charge of the books?'

'Since our accountant complained about the army of ants which kept running riot over the pages,' she quipped, accurately describing her brother's atrocious handwriting.

Now Lucas shot her a quizzical look. 'Still that bad, hmm?'

She laughed, and caught his acknowledging smile. Her breath lodged in her throat. Lethal, she thought, not for the first time. 'He should have been a doctor,' she declared, filing another folder, sorting a mis-file at the same time.

'And whilst you're designing boats and keeping the accounts, what does Dan do?' Lucas enquired mildly.

It was on the tip of her tongue to say, Spends money we can ill afford to lose, but thought better of it. 'Daniel is in charge of promotion. Somebody has to go out there and get people to buy,' she explained, wondering just what the two men had talked about these last few days. Certainly not Terrell's, by the sound of it.

As she reached for the next folder, she found that Lucas had crossed the room silently and was there before her. His hand skimmed off the file and opened it for his lazy perusal. Fortunately it was only the sailmaker's account, so he wouldn't learn much from it. She sent him a speaking look, which, naturally, he ignored.

'That doesn't sound like Dan's sort of job to me,' Lucas observed, and she grimaced.

'No, he'd much rather be out on the water, but he knows this is just the beginning. We're all dependent on each other. I design the boats, Ted will build them, and when we've made enough money Daniel will race them.' It was perfect. Daniel had always craved thrills and excitement, and this idea had really set him buzzing.

'Sounds ideal,' Lucas conceded. 'So why do I get the feeling there's a "but" in there somewhere?'

Megan saw no point in beating about the bush. 'It's all taking a little longer than we expected,' she admitted ruefully.

Lucas didn't need it spelling out to him. 'And Dan's beginning to get restless,' he pronounced, tossing the file back on the pile.

'I was hoping spending time with you would recharge his batteries,' she said, although she doubted it after their latest row.

'Perhaps this afternoon will help. We're taking the *Sea Mist* out for a run.'

The mention of the yacht their father had built brought a glow to her eyes. She had nothing but happy memories of golden days spent on the water. 'She could do with it. I'd give a fortune to be going with you!' she exclaimed wistfully, and Lucas smiled down at her.

'Why don't you? There's plenty of room.'

Tempted, Megan looked up right into his eyes, and had the distinct impression that she was already on the water—and in danger of drowning! In the next instant she was shaking her head and taking a step backwards. Boy, oh, boy! No wonder women toppled like ninepins. His charisma was breathtaking. It had certainly acquired the unhappy knack of stealing her breath away!

'Daniel wouldn't like it. Besides, I have too much to

do here,' she said, abandoning the filing to take her seat behind the desk. 'Is that what you came to tell me?'

'Partly. I actually came to ask you to have dinner with me.'

If she'd been given a million years to think, she never would have come up with that. 'Been stood up, have you?' she asked, not bothering to hide her amusement at the idea.

Lucas's eyes took on a gleam of devilment and he didn't deny it. 'Keep me company and you can gloat to your heart's content,' he offered.

Megan sat back and crossed her arms, liking the idea of enjoying herself at his expense. 'Well, well, who would have thought that the Don Juan of Europe would be so strapped for company that he would be forced to ask me for a date?' she exclaimed, deciding she also liked the way his eyes sparkled with amusement.

Lucas grinned, and whimsically she felt she could understand how Red Riding Hood must have felt on first encountering the wolf! 'Of course, if you're too scared to agree, Red...' he began, and her brows rose.

'Are you actually daring me, Lucas?' she asked softly, and he laughed low in his throat.

'Would I?'

Since when had he had a voice like rich, dark chocolate? she wondered with a tiny shiver. 'You'd do anything if it was to your advantage,' she said baldly, and he laughed again.

'Is that a yes or a no?'

'It's neither. I'm wondering why you haven't asked my brother,' she hedged neatly.

'I did, but Dan's got a prior engagement.'

So much for hoping that spending time with his old friend would wean him away from the new! Though her heart sank, she made her voice light. 'In that case

I'd better take pity on you, hadn't I? On one condition, though.'

His lips twitched as he suppressed a smile. 'Which is?'

'That we go somewhere there won't be any cameras. I don't want to wake up tomorrow to find my photograph splashed across the tabloids and me described as your latest woman!' she proposed drily.

Lucas inclined his head. 'I promise you the utmost discretion. And if by chance a reporter should turn up I'll insist that we're just good friends,' he retorted, tongue-in-cheek, and Megan groaned.

'Don't do me any favours!' she snapped, and he laughed as he headed for the door.

'I'll see you in the hall at eight.'

Megan closed her eyes, aware that she was looking forward to the evening more than she would have expected. A bubbling laugh escaped as she grinned to herself. It would be interesting to see just how the Lucas Canfield machine went into operation.

At a quarter to eight that evening, Megan made her way downstairs. She stopped before the hall mirror, and smiled at what she saw. She had taken great care with her appearance, an imp of mischief making her pull out all the stops. After all, it wasn't every day that a woman was taken out by the legendary Lucas Canfield! She had braided her wild mop of hair into a French plait, which drew attention to the delicate structure of her cheeks and jaw. Then, using the minimal amount of make-up to the greatest effect, she had turned her eyes into mysterious green pools, and given her lips that just kissed pinkness.

She had chosen to wear her little black dress, with its tiny straps and figure-hugging lines, because it flattered her and gave her skin the creaminess of alabaster. She hoped it would knock his eyes out, and felt a kick of excitement at the idea.

Hearing a door slam upstairs, Megan darted away from the mirror, not wanting to be caught preening. She made her way through to the kitchen at the back of the house. Ted was at the sink washing up his dinner things. He lived in a cottage just down the lane, but a fire had virtually gutted his own kitchen a month ago, and Megan had insisted he use theirs until the rebuilding was done. As he was doing the work himself, he turned up at odd hours to eat the supper she left for him in the microwave.

He glanced round, eyes widening when he saw how she was dressed. 'Where are you off to?'

Megan pulled out a chair and sat down at the table. 'I'm going out to dinner with the world's sexiest man. According to several magazine polls, he has the wickedest smile and the cutest backside,' she told him, grinning as his brows rose.

Ted sniffed. 'Sounds like a prat to me!'

Megan giggled, feeling more exhilarated and expectant than she had for a very long time. 'You've no soul, Ted. Nine out of ten women would have recognised Lucas from that description.'

'Lucas?' Ted's startled expression crinkled into a grin. 'I bet that made him spitting mad,' he declared, and they both burst out laughing.

'It's his fault for getting such a reputation,' Megan pronounced. 'Do you remember what it was like before he left? No woman was safe!'

Ted sobered. 'Aye, I remember, so just you be careful, girl. I'd hate to see you get hurt.'

Megan was warmed by his caring. 'Lucas can't hurt me,' she reassured him.

He raised a soapy hand warningly. 'Any woman can get hurt. You're no exception.'

There were all sorts of hurts, but the one he worried

about was the one least likely to affect her. She kept her own counsel, though, and went over and squeezed his arm. 'Don't worry, I'll be careful,' she promised. 'Anyway, Lucas and I are like chalk and cheese. We never agree about anything.'

'People who say that usually end up married to each other!' Ted pointed out humorously, and her smile faltered just a little.

'Not us. I don't ever intend to get married,' she said firmly, but he only shook his head.

'Who knows what the future has in store for us?'

Megan turned away, masking the bleakness in her eyes with lowered lashes. 'Who knows?' she repeated shortly. She knew. Had known it since she was eighteen years old. Nothing had changed, nor ever could. There was no mystery, just plain, cold fact.

She shivered and glanced up, staring straight into a pair of shocking blue eyes which were regarding her oddly. Her nerves leapt and her throat closed over. Lucas had appeared from out of nowhere.

'Are you practising for the SAS or something?' she snapped, jerked out of her calm by his silent approach. Why did he have to creep about the place like that?

'Next time I'll cough loudly to announce my presence,' Lucas declared drily, walking over to Ted with his hand held out. 'Good to see you again, Ted.'

This was the first time their paths had crossed since Lucas had arrived, and Ted responded with a smile and a grip like a clam. 'You too, Lucas. Looks like you've done well for yourself.'

'I can't complain.' He nodded towards the sink. 'I see Red has got you well trained.'

Ted scowled. 'This is all she'll let me do. I had a small fire back at my cottage, and she insists I eat here until it's repaired. Won't take any money, so the washing-up is mine.' He sent her a glare which was supposed to remind her that he was still angry about not paying his way.

Megan narrowed her eyes back at him. 'I have to cook anyway, so don't say another word. I want to do this.'

Ted's expression softened. 'You're a right mother hen, fussing over me like I'm your only chick. What you need is a family of your own to cluck over.'

Megan knew he meant it kindly, and didn't know how his words hurt her. Nor would she reveal it. If her smile didn't reach her eyes, he didn't know it. 'I've enough to do with you and Daniel,' she quipped, and turned pointedly to Lucas. 'We're going to be late,' she warned, and Ted rolled his eyes.

'Uh-oh. When she gets that look in her eye, a wise man heads for cover. You'd better come down to the yard for a talk, Lucas. It's been a long time since we had a chat.'

'Too long,' Lucas agreed. 'I'll be there.'

'Look forward to it,' Ted nodded. 'Now, it wouldn't do to keep the lady waiting any longer.'

'Not when she's got a temper on her to match her hair,' Lucas agreed, and stood aside to allow Megan to lead the way out.

'I'll lock up on my way out, Megan,' Ted called after her.

'OK, Ted. See you tomorrow.' Pausing in the hall to collect her shawl and bag from where she had left them on a side table, she turned to find Lucas looking her up and down with masculine appreciation. Prickles danced over her skin, and to hide it she summoned up a dose of mockery. 'I hope you approve. I didn't want to ruin your reputation by appearing dowdy.'

His blue eyes danced. 'I'm impressed. I won't have eyes for any other woman tonight,' he declared smoothly, and although Megan had heard the same words any number of times on this occasion she found that it brought her out in goose-bumps.

Masking her surprise with the ease of long practice at hiding her feelings, she let her own gaze study him. Lucas was. . .heart-stopping. The dinner suit did with subtlety what jeans did so blatantly: hint at the latent power of the muscular body beneath. No wonder women queued up to go out with him. He was all male, pure power and virility.

And, however much it went against the grain, she knew in all honesty that she wasn't proof against it. She was strongly attracted. He appealed to her on a physical level, but that was nothing new. Attraction was one thing, doing something about it entirely another. She had common sense enough to know that there would never be anything between herself and Lucas. It was inconceivable, she thought with a whimsical smile.

'I'm sure you're already aware that you look as handsome as sin,' she quipped as she let herself out of the door and waited for him to join her.

'Does that mean you think I'm vain?' he asked ironically, taking her elbow and steering her down the path to where his classic Jaguar waited.

Megan laughed and met his blue gaze. 'I would never be so rude. Besides, vanity is in the eye of the beholder!'

His expression became quizzical. 'I thought that was beauty?'

She allowed her lips to curve wryly. 'It all depends on your perspective. What *you* see when you look in the mirror might be beauty, and therefore vanity, whilst what *I* see when I look at you is entirely different,' she proclaimed brightly, and felt warmth bubble up inside her when he laughed.

'God help me, I know I'm going to regret it, but I have to ask. What *do* you see?' Lucas challenged as he reached round to open the passenger door for her.

Amusement danced in her eyes as she turned to survey him with every appearance of seriousness. 'You're quite good-looking, in a...battered sort of way.'

Lucas winced. 'You make me sound like an old suitcase that's gone round the world one too many times! I have to hand it to you, Red, you certainly know how to cut a man down to size.'

'It's good for your ego,' she declared humorously. 'Somebody has to make sure you don't believe all that flattery,' she added, climbing inside the car and taking an appreciative glance round at the handsome interior.

'So you've appointed yourself the guardian of my morals?' he queried mildly, shutting the door and going round to take his own seat.

Megan fastened her seat belt. 'Why not? I've always seen you very clearly.' She'd never been blinded to his faults by his good looks and charm.

Starting the car, he cast a brief glance at her before pulling out into the road. 'And disliked what you saw.'

Megan watched his hands on the wheel. They were very competent. She had no doubts about him handling the powerful car. Whatever he did had his full attention—even his women! 'I won't be a hypocrite and deny that you're good to look at. It's your attitude towards women that leaves something to be desired.'

Lucas took his eyes from the road for a second, sending her a grin. 'I thought the trouble was that I desired them all!' he taunted, before concentrating on his driving once more.

She sent him an exasperated look. 'Don't you have any conscience at all?'

'Apparently not. What I need is a Jiminy Cricket. Care to take on the job?'

'No, thanks. It would be a thankless task, with very little job satisfaction. You'd never listen.'

He chuckled. 'Perhaps you underestimate yourself.'

Megan shook her head. 'I have no influence on you.'

'Probably because you're going about it the wrong way. Try cajolery instead of a blunt weapon,' Lucas advised, causing her to turn and study his profile to see whether he was serious or not. There were crinkles beside his eyes and mouth which told her he wasn't.

'Now you're spoiling my fantasies!' she complained. 'I had visions of you stretched unconscious at my feet.'

'Well, now, if we're swapping fantasies—' Lucas began wickedly, and she interrupted him swiftly.

'We're not,' she declared repressively, which only made him laugh.

'Coward.'

Megan found herself smiling as she turned to look out of the window. Catching her reflection, she sighed. Damn him. Even when she had been seriously disgusted with him, he'd always managed to make her laugh. It was so irritating!

'So, tell me, Red, what have you been doing with yourself these last eight years?' Lucas asked, after a while.

'You mean besides blighting the lives of all the local men?' she countered sardonically, and he shot her a narrow-eyed look.

'It's all a joke to you, isn't it?' he condemned shortly, and Megan shrugged.

Of course it wasn't, but she wasn't about to explain why. Instead she said musingly, 'I find it strange that if a man had made a similar statement about women you'd merely have laughed. Do I detect a double standard?'

Lucas didn't take his eyes from the road. 'I wouldn't have laughed,' he said firmly, and Megan snorted sceptically.

'Says the man who goes through women like a hot knife through butter! How you ever manage to fit in work heaven only knows. I'm assuming, that is, that you do work?' she goaded drily.

'Oh, I manage to write the odd letter or two.'

She looked at him mockingly. 'You mean you can remember what pen and paper are? I should be careful—you might overdo it and have to retire to bed!'

Lucas chuckled, a rich sound which made her flesh tingle most unsettlingly. 'If I had to retire to bed, I wouldn't go alone,' he informed her.

'That I can believe. I'm sure Sonja would oblige,' she drawled, recalling the woman's. . .eagerness.

'I'm sure she would,' he agreed silkily, a reminiscent smile curving his lips. 'However, being an airline hostess, she might well be on the other side of the world, so I'd have to find a substitute.'

'There shouldn't be any shortage of those! The queue would probably outdo Harrods' January sale!'

'It's nice to hear you think so highly of my. . . prowess,' Lucas came back softly, and she couldn't help but laugh.

'Sorry to disillusion you, Lucas, but it isn't that I think highly of you, rather that the IQ of the women you take out has got to be in single figures!' she countered smartly, but only succeeded in making him grin.

'You're never short of a sharp remark, are you, Red? You'd better be careful you don't cut yourself. After all, I'm taking you out tonight, so what does that say about your IQ?'

Megan waved a hand airily. 'That doesn't count. For one thing, I'm not blonde. More importantly, dining with you seemed slightly more enjoyable than cleaning the oven—a chore I'll put off at the slightest excuse.'

His soft laugh set the hairs rising on her skin. 'You know something, Red? You're one of the few women who can genuinely amuse me.'

Her eyebrows shot up. 'Really? I thought I made you angry.'

'You do that too. Your cavalier handling of men is hardly likely to endear me.'

'Ditto your use of women,' she returned coolly.

'So we have something in common after all,' he responded mildly, turning the car into the drive of a very exclusive country club.

Not quite, she thought. His actions had no purpose other than his own pleasure, whilst hers were a necessity. She would not raise false hopes, even if sometimes she felt very lonely indeed.

She stared up at the ivy-clad structure. It looked very expensive, the sort of establishment you had to be a member of to visit. 'I didn't know this place existed,' she murmured as they parked in the first available space.

Lucas turned to her with a faint frown as he switched off the engine. 'Dan recommended it. I assumed you'd been here before.'

Megan felt her face tighten. If Daniel frequented this sort of place, no wonder they were in trouble. Her heart sank, even as she managed to stop her smile from slipping. 'He must wine and dine potential customers here. Now I know why his expense account is so huge!' she joked, though joking was very far from her mind. To suspect the sort of place her brother was using was one thing, to know, another. She climbed out of the car knowing she would always have this picture in her mind now.

Lucas joined her, taking her elbow in a firm hold but not immediately making a move to enter the building. 'You've gone very quiet. Is something wrong?'

She could have groaned. Didn't he miss anything? 'I was marvelling at the lengths you've gone to for one little meal,' she taunted, and began walking towards the front door.

Lucas fell into step beside her. 'Impressed?'

'It's quite taken my breath away!' she exclaimed drolly, and he gave a bark of laughter.

'Good. It means I'll be spared your particular brand of sparkling repartee for a while,' Lucas shot back pithily, making Megan smile.

'How unkind! Not to mention ungentlemanly!' she complained, her eyes recovering some of their lost sparkle.

'You have the knack of making me forget to be a gentleman. However, I ease my conscience with the knowledge that there are times when you're very far from being a lady,' Lucas returned smartly.

She suspected a double meaning, but chose to ignore it. 'I'll have you know I stopped climbing trees years ago.'

'That's a shame. I used to enjoy catching a glimpse of your long legs in those very short shorts you used to wear!' He sighed regretfully, really stealing her breath this time. When he glanced at her, his eyes gleamed like the devil. 'You have, as the Americans would say, legs to die for.'

Megan felt those selfsame legs turn decidedly wobbly as they walked inside. She knew he had said it on purpose to put her off balance, but even so it made her feel hot inside to know that he admired her legs. She sought her brain for a snappy reply, but a man in evening dress came to meet them and the moment was lost.

'Good evening, sir, madam. You'll be dining?'

Lucas relieved Megan of her shawl and handed it to the man. 'I've a table booked for eight-thirty.'

'The restaurant is to your left. I hope you enjoy your meal.' He nodded at them both and disappeared.

Lucas glanced towards an archway from which issued bursts of laughter. 'The bar sounds crowded. We'll go straight to our table, unless you object?'

Megan was happy to accede to his idea. She had
recovered her poise now, and was determined to get
her own back. Lucas's teasing had always managed to
find a way through her defences when they were young,
and it appeared that eight years had made no difference. However, she was no longer a child, and her
weapons were sharper. She was determined to give as
good as she got.

The restaurant turned out to be part of a nightclub.
Discreetly lit tables encircled a dance area which
already had one or two couples gliding around to the
music of a live band. Around the walls, plants and
partitions gave some tables a semblance of privacy.
Perfect for lovers, she mused wryly, and wasn't surprised to follow the waiter to a secluded table.

'We have the champagne you ordered chilling, sir,'
he told them as soon as they were seated. 'I can serve
it now, unless the lady would prefer something else?'

Lucas quirked an eyebrow her way. 'Megan?'

'The lady would like a stinger, please.'

Lucas ordered a Manhattan for himself, and the
waiter nodded, handed each a large padded menu and
departed. As soon as they were alone, Megan set her
elbows on the table and rested her chin on her cupped
hands. The Lucas Canfield machine had just gone into
motion, and it brought a wry twist to her lips. He was
certainly smooth. The result of years of practice.

'Champagne? All this undivided attention could
quite easily go to a girl's head if she wasn't careful.'

Lucas sat forward, so that the room between them
was drastically reduced. 'Ah, but we both know how
careful you are, Red. When it comes to the warmer
emotions, your head will ever rule your heart.'

It wasn't said to be unkind. To Lucas it was a simple
statement of fact. How could he know that it was only
true because there were some risks she was not prepared to take? Someone had to be strong. To say

enough was enough. It ended here, with her, and to hell with what anyone else thought!

Megan met Lucas's steady blue gaze. 'Are you sure?'

'I'm never sure of women. They can always surprise me,' he returned drily.

'Even me?'

'Let's just say I know you better than most women, so it would be highly unlikely.'

'How diplomatic of you,' she laughed, allowing her attention to drift around the room. 'I suppose you take all your women to places like this?' she remarked as she encountered a ferocious glare from a bottle blonde sitting a few tables away. She was taken aback at first, but her eyes swiftly began to dance with amused speculation. 'Tell me, are you forever running into old flames? Like that one over there?' Megan tipped her head in the blonde's direction.

Lucas took a brief glance round. 'Ah.'

Sensing a problem, she raised her brows and smiled sweetly. '"Ah"?' Mentally rubbing her hands, she waited for what she expected would be a jealous confrontation.

Lucas was fully aware of her enjoyment. 'That's Mona, a friend of Sonja's.'

The penny dropped and her smiled widened. 'Oh, I see. You had a date with her tonight, didn't you? And you cancelled it, saying. . .?'

His teeth gleamed whitely as he smiled back unrepentantly. 'That I had a business meeting.'

Megan decided that the evening had just gained added appeal. 'And Mona now knows it wasn't and will tell Sonja. My, you do have a problem, don't you? I had no idea how exciting a rakish lifestyle could be.' She made no attempt to hide her glee, and her sympathy was loaded with irony. 'Is there anything I can do to help? Do you want me to go and explain that I'm just a good friend?'

Observing her with some amusement, Lucas put up a restraining hand. 'Spare us. I can do my own explaining. I know how to handle women like Sonja.'

Megan's smile took on a scornful curve. 'I wouldn't doubt it for a second. Lord knows, you've had enough practice.'

Lucas's reply was thwarted by the arrival of their drinks, and he had to wait until the waiter had gone to respond. 'Considering your own less than perfect treatment of men, do you think you have the right to be so disapproving, Red?'

She might have guessed he would throw that in her face. 'I don't use men the way you use women, Lucas. You care no more for them than you do for your car,' she condemned, but that only produced a wider smile.

'On the contrary, I see my car as a work of art, and treat it accordingly,' he corrected smoothly, making her hackles rise.

Of all the arrogantly chauvinistic remarks she had ever heard, that took the cake! 'Women are more than bodies to be polished and admired!' she retorted scornfully, then caught the gleam in his eye which told her he had deliberately thrown out the bait she had taken so easily.

Lucas watched the heat die out of her. 'You do like to lead with your chin, don't you?'

He was as slippery as a snake, and he knew her too well! 'That doesn't alter the fact that your reputation hardly does you credit.'

'I'm not responsible for what the Press choose to write, or for what you choose to believe,' he told her levelly, sipping at his drink.

'Meaning that the reports of your prowess have been greatly exaggerated?' she challenged, and his blue eyes gleamed devilishly.

'How can I answer that without sounding big-headed? Let's just say when I want a woman to purr she does.'

Though she knew darn well he was goading her, Megan felt a shiver run down her spine, and disgust had nothing to do with it. He had a way of saying and doing things which played havoc with her senses. She savoured her own drink before attempting a reply.

'Just remember, cats that purr also have claws. You're going to come a cropper one day.' And how she'd like to be there to see it!

'Something tells me I shouldn't look to you for solace when the time comes,' he remarked, with wry amusement.

Megan opened her mouth to agree, but a discreet cough announced the arrival of the waiter once more. 'Would you care to order now, sir?'

Lucas picked up the menu and raised an eyebrow at her. 'Shall I order for you?' he asked, and Megan nodded. Usually she preferred to choose herself, but it would be interesting to see what Lucas would pick out. He reeled off a selection in the original French, and within minutes the waiter had disappeared as silently as he had come.

Megan was impressed in spite of herself. He did it all so naturally that he commanded respect from staff who were long past being impressed. 'Do you always order for your dates?' She couldn't believe that women really liked having the choice taken away from them.

Lucas sat back, the better to observe her. 'Only when asked to. I don't force myself on women in any fashion.'

It pleased her to hear it, and, really, she hadn't expected him to be that sort anyway. It didn't stop her provoking him, though. 'I thought you might be afraid I would order the most expensive dishes.'

'Would you have?' he challenged, and Megan dropped her gaze to her glass for a moment before meeting his eyes again, her own revealing amused honesty.

'I admit to being tempted, but I decided that being ill would harm me more than your pocket, so if you've chosen oysters, smoked salmon or caviare they'll have to go back because I don't like them,' she informed him lightly, taking another sip of her drink.

There was a certain fondness in the smile he gave her. 'I'm glad you finally learned not to cut off your nose to spite your face. You can relax, Megan. I seem to recall you were always partial to fish, so I ordered Dover sole.'

Megan sighed. If she was noting his faults, she would have a very short list! 'You speak French very well.'

His face softened. 'I had a good teacher. And, before you ask, yes, it was a woman, and no, not in the way you mean. My mother was half-French, and she insisted I learn both languages as a child. Then I spent my holidays with her mother, my grandmother, when I was allowed to speak nothing but French. Fortunately I found it easy, and as I grew older I discovered I had a knack for languages. Which came in handy when expanding our market into Europe.'

Megan listened with genuine interest, vaguely recalling a very elegant woman who used to call for Lucas sometimes. 'I think I remember your mother. She was very beautiful.'

'She still is, though her hair is more grey now.'

'I recall your parents left the area soon after you did. Wasn't your father some sort of scientist?' Like most children, what she had known of her friends' families had been sketchy at best.

'He was a research chemist. Very hush-hush. He died several years ago, and my mother decided to go back to France. As my work takes me abroad regularly, I see more of her now than I used to. She's happy, but she misses Dad. They had a good marriage. I envy them that.'

She saw the way his face softened, and felt as if her heart was being squeezed. For a fleeting instant she saw herself with the sort of marriage he meant. Saw herself loving and being loved. With children and shared laughter. Things she hadn't allowed herself to think of for a very long time. She felt their loss so keenly, she wanted to cry. Only by biting her lip did she manage to blink away the threatening moisture. She didn't have time for this, and 'what if's were pointless. They were no match for facts, and that was what she had. Cold, hard, ruthless facts — and the strength of will to do what was right.

It was that same indomitable strength which had her raising her glass with a smile. 'A toast. To happy families,' she declared with a toss of her head, and drained the little which remained in her glass.

Lucas followed suit, but his expression was dubious. 'I thought you didn't believe in such things?'

Megan studied her empty glass, recalling clearly the conversation they had had that first night. 'Of course I believe in them, for other people. I intend to remain independent.'

'Free of encumbrances?'

A faint smile twisted her lips. 'Don't sound so disapproving. You're still unencumbered and you're older than I am!' she exclaimed lightly, though, as always, the mention of family made her heart heavy.

'I told you — I haven't found the right woman yet,' Lucas countered easily.

Megan gave an unladylike snort. 'Not for want of trying! Oh, Lucas, you can't really expect me to believe you're a romantic?'

His blue eyes glittered back at her. 'I've warned you before about jumping to conclusions about me.'

She looked sceptical. 'Yes, but love. . .'

'Love has been known to move mountains.'

'So has dynamite!' she quipped back instantly, but he remained serious.

'Laugh if you want to, but, whether they admit it or not, everyone needs love.'

Megan's heart gave a painful lurch. Oh, yes, she needed love. Sometimes she felt so lonely, it was as if she had an aching void inside her. Then she would recall why she would never fill it, and painfully she would shore up her defences.

Now she hid her resignation behind an incredulous smile. 'Even you?'

Lucas inclined his head gravely. 'Even me. I know that, if I keep looking one day I will find the one woman I'll want to share my life with,' he admitted easily, and his sincerity was something she couldn't argue with.

She was shaken, she admitted to herself, and because of it she couldn't find it in her to mock him. Though it went against all she knew of him, she believed him. And the knowledge brought an unknown wistfulness to the curve of her lips as she stared at him. 'I hope you find her, Lucas,' she said gruffly, then, uncomfortably aware that he was looking at her oddly, she made a business of looking round for the waiter. 'I'm starving. Aren't you?' she declared over-brightly.

'Thank you,' Lucas said softly, and she sent him a startled look.

'What for?'

There was a strange expression in his eyes which she couldn't name. 'For being honest.'

Colour washed into her cheeks. 'I. . .' She stopped her instinctive denial and sighed. 'You meant it, and I couldn't step on your dreams,' she said truthfully.

'You could have done. I find it interesting that you didn't.'

'Well, don't read anything into it which isn't there. I

had a noble impulse. Don't make me regret it,' she warned shortly. She didn't want him probing into her motives. Lucas had the sort of incisive brain which cut through masking trivia to the important matter hiding inside. He could easily discover her armour for what it was, and then he would go on to destroy it in order to find what she was hiding.

That must not happen. For what would be amusing to him would devastate her. Her armour was all she had, and she would protect it to her last breath. She wanted no man's pity, and especially not Lucas's!

CHAPTER FOUR

WHETHER Lucas had taken Megan's hint or not, he turned out to be an ideal dinner companion. He put himself out to relax and amuse her, and it wasn't long before her equilibrium returned and she found herself enjoying both the food and the company.

The conversation became lively as they went from topic to topic. Much to her surprise, Megan discovered they had the same taste in music and literature. Her guard dropped, and for the first time in what seemed like for ever she found she was really enjoying herself. When he launched into a series of anecdotes told with a dry, sometimes wicked sense of humour, laughter bubbled out of her.

She realised with a pang that she had missed his sense of humour. He was telling her about a friend of his who had come to grief on a skiing trip, and she found herself watching the way his eyes crinkled up as he laughed, and listening to the dark magic of his voice. His eyes danced, inviting her to share the joke. He laughed with pure enjoyment and her heart began a crazy dance in her chest.

Simultaneously warning flares went off in her brain, and with a sense of incredulity Megan became aware that she was in very real danger of falling under the spell of his charm. The dismaying thing was that he had won her over without even trying, because Megan Terrell was no more than the proverbial thorn in his side. The sister of his best friend. A pest.

The knowledge sobered her. She didn't need the complications of a one-sided attraction. She didn't want to be attracted at all. But she was, and she had only one way of dealing with it. She must ignore it. Starved of fuel, the feeling would die a natural death. Helped by the fact that Lucas did not feel the same attraction. Aware of the danger, she could remain on the outside looking in, and enjoy the show.

When the sweet trolley arrived, Megan was once more in control of her wayward senses. With her brain fully functioning, she allowed Lucas to choose for her, accepting the generous slice of chocolate gateau with a wry laugh.

He glanced at her with brows raised. 'Something wrong?'

'Not really. I was laughing because I think I've discovered how you do it,' she explained lightly.

'It?'

With a long-suffering sigh, Megan rested her chin on one hand and sent him a smile. 'Trap usually intelligent women. First you flatter their egos with single-minded attention, next you disarm them with laughter, and finally you seduce them with the sensual delight of food. Very simple. Very effective,' she enlightened him breezily as she cut a spoonful of cake and raised it to her lips.

She had to admire the swiftness of his brain. After a fleeting instant of surprise, Lucas looked across at her with eyes full of appreciative humour. 'I had no idea you were taking notes.'

'I'm thinking of writing a book. You know the sort of thing. *Seduction—the Canfield Way.*'

'I'm sure you can find a better subject for study than myself,' he argued, watching her enjoyment through hooded eyes.

Megan held up her hand. 'There's no need to be so modest. I imagine you have a very low failure rate,' she insisted, warming to the idea, hoping to discomfit him. Toying with another spoonful of the delicious cake, she began to raise it to her mouth. Halfway, she happened to glance across the table, and discovered that Lucas was watching the manoeuvre with an intensity which gave her an odd little thrill, chasing her breath away and increasing the beat of her heart.

It was then that an imp of devilment took hold of her, for, instead of retreating, she carried the spoonful to her mouth, deliberately savouring the texture on her tongue. She waited, scarcely breathing as a rush of excitement kicked in her stomach, then he transferred his gaze to her eyes. Wry amusement didn't quite mask the sensual warmth she saw there.

He sat back, crossing his legs comfortably. 'Taste good?' he asked huskily.

'Delicious,' she conceded, wondering if she had taken leave of her senses. Those were not the sort of games you played with a man like Lucas.

'You're a tease,' he accused, with a shake of his head.

'And you're an unprincipled flirt,' she responded instantly.

He grinned. 'Some would say in that case we deserve each other.'

Megan raised her brows pointedly. 'It's a proven fact that very few people get what they deserve. If they did, you would have been boiled in oil long ago!'

'You're a bloodthirsty little thing, aren't you?' Lucas marvelled. 'Beautiful but bloodthirsty.'

Though her brain urged caution, she found she was enjoying the exchange too much to stop. 'Ah, a compliment. Should I swoon?'

Lucas's lips twitched. 'I wouldn't advise it.'

'I thought your women were expected to keel over on command?' she challenged mockingly.

He rubbed a thoughtful finger along the bridge of his nose. 'It's optional. For myself, I'd hate to see you flop face first into your chocolate cake.'

Megan couldn't stop the laugh which gurgled out of

her. 'You have a point. Perhaps I should start purring instead?' she asked dulcetly.

His blue eyes glittered brightly as he studied her mobile face, which was alight with mischief. 'Only if you want to,' he said softly.

She sighed, abandoning the sweet and wiping her lips with her napkin. 'The trouble is, I never did manage to master the technique of doing that. Sorry. You'll just have to wait for Sonja to oblige.'

He didn't have to laugh; the way his eyes glittered was proof enough of his amusement. 'It wouldn't be the same. There is an alternative. Perhaps I could teach you to purr?'

The *double entendre* made her nerves leap. 'I wouldn't put you to so much trouble.'

'Oh, it wouldn't be a bother, it would be a pleasure,' he riposted silkily, clearly enjoying himself, and Megan found to her surprise that she liked amusing him.

'Mmm,' she acknowledged drily. 'That's what I thought!'

This time Lucas laughed aloud, studying her as if he had never quite seen her before. 'Having fun?' he asked at last, and Megan sighed.

'Actually, I haven't enjoyed myself so much for a long time,' she admitted, and knew, with a sense of despair, that it was true. Trying to keep Terrell's afloat took all her energy, so that she had little left for enjoyment these days.

'Hmm, I'd take that as a compliment if your enjoyment wasn't at my expense,' Lucas responded sardonically. 'However, I'm prepared to overlook it if you dance with me,' he offered as he stood up.

She supposed she should have taken umbrage at his assumption of her acceptance, but Megan saw no real reason to refuse. She loved dancing, and she had every reason to suppose that Lucas was a good dancer, seeing as he had taught her in the first place. Besides, it was only a dance. She rose to her feet.

'Don't tread on my toes,' she warned teasingly.

He smiled into her eyes. 'Trust me,' he said, and led her onto the floor.

The thought that struck her as she turned to him was that she did trust Lucas. He was one of the most trustworthy men she knew. She was warmed by the knowledge as he drew her into his arms, and as a consequence her defences were lowered, heightening her perception of herself and the man who held her.

She knew at once that this was different. She had danced countless times with her hand on a man's shoulder, his arm braced around her, guiding her. She had been held close, so that there was scarcely room for a wisp of air to pass between their two bodies. Yet this was not the same. It was light years from being the same.

Awareness took on a totally new dimension. Slowly her fingers flexed, taking in the texture of the cloth which stretched across the broad span of his shoulders. Lucas was strong and powerful; he made her conscious of her own softer curves being flattened against him.

A tiny sigh escaped her lips as something very basic struck her. Their bodies fitted together so well, it was as if they had been made for each other. She felt protected, sheltered, and knew that there was nothing in this world she would rather do than rest her head on the shoulder which lay so invitingly close. Something expanded inside her, and without thought her eyelids fluttered down, and at once her body softened, melting against his as she drifted with the music.

When she felt his hand move in a lazy glide up her spine, pressing her closer, she wanted to sigh. Nothing had ever felt so right.

Lost to the world, she barely registered Lucas's muffled, 'Hell!' an instant before somebody cannoned into her from behind, making her eyes fly open as she stumbled. Lucas prevented her from falling with a fearsome grip on her arm. She would have bruises tomorrow, she mused wryly. Glancing around, she realised the floor had filled up, and she hadn't been aware of it.

'Are you OK?' he asked, glancing down at her, and Megan nodded.

'Where did all these people come from?'

Lucas looked amused. 'I had the feeling you were nodding off,' he teased, then frowned as they were bumped again. 'This is impossible,' he muttered tersely. 'We'd better go back to our table.'

Megan was happy to fall in with the suggestion. Her mind was whirling as they struggled through the milling couples. She hadn't been nodding off—she had been miles away. Lucas had felt so safe that she had been able to forget her fears and worries for a small moment of time. He'd always been good at that, so there was nothing to get alarmed about, she told herself. She had simply been able to relax because she had known he would make no demands on her. There was nothing else to read into it. Nothing at all.

All the same, she decided it would be a good time to take a break. It was very hot inside, and she needed to cool down anyway. So when they reached their table she didn't sit down, but picked up her bag.

'I'm just going to freshen up,' she explained when she met his questioning look. 'Why don't you order some more drinks? I won't be long,' she promised as she turned and walked away.

Crossing the busy foyer, Megan was searching for the right door, when a roar of male laughter from above made her glance up. A group of men stood on the landing, her brother amongst them. Of course she now knew that Daniel came here, but, with the night-club downstairs, what could there be on the first floor to hold his interest? This could be her first clue as to what was troubling him, she realised, and she altered course to mount the sweeping staircase, determined to find out.

As she reached the landing, the group began to disperse into a room to their left. Hurrying after them, she caught Daniel's arm before he disappeared. He turned at once, surprise turning to horror when he saw her.

'What the hell are you doing here?' he demanded in a shaken tone, and her heart sank as she examined his ashen face.

'I was about to ask you the same thing,' she said huskily, aware of a nameless anxiety clawing at her. What was wrong?

One of the other men had turned in the doorway. 'Come on, Danny; stop nattering and get yourself in here. We've no time for skirts tonight!' he ordered, giving Megan a cursory glance of dislike before vanishing inside.

She had met him once and the dislike was mutual. '*Danny*?' she queried disbelievingly, and Daniel coloured angrily.

'It's what my friends call me.'

Considering he had hated that diminutive all his life, she was surprised he allowed the use of it. 'If they were your friends, they'd know you hate the name.'

'Don't start, Megan. It's only a name, so why should I let it spoil my fun?'

Megan felt her throat close over, too aware of her anxiety to be angry. 'Fun is supposed to make you happy, Daniel, not like this. Won't you please come home and talk to me, tell me what's wrong?' she pleaded, and felt him tense under her hand.

Daniel's jaw clenched mutinously. 'There's nothing wrong. How many times have I got to tell you that how I live my life is my business?'

Her thumbs were pricking badly, and she knew she had to replace her burgeoning anger with reason. 'Not just yours. You're squandering away everything our family worked so hard to build.'

A guilty colour stained his cheeks at that. 'So what? Terrell's is mine now, and I can choose to do what I want with the proceeds.'

Which reminded her of something she hadn't had time to tell him. She'd been waiting for an appropriate moment, but there was no time like the present — if it would help. 'There might not be any proceeds much longer. The German cancelled his order,' she said bluntly.

There was a second when he seemed to sway, but then he had control of himself once more. Only his voice held a betraying quiver. 'That's his prerogative.'

Her anger was despairing. 'And you don't give a damn!'

Daniel laughed raggedly, shaking off her hand. 'You're wasting your time trying to make me feel guilty, Meg,' he told her shortly. 'I suppose Lucas brought you here, so why don't you go back to him and stop spying on me?' he ordered. Turning his back, he walked into the room and shut the door on her.

Megan stared at the silent wood in shock, her mind filled with the brief but telling glimpse she had caught of well-patronised gaming tables. Gambling. Her blood ran cold, and she realised she was trembling. Daniel wasn't just living beyond his means, he was gambling! Not penny ante stuff, but the real thing. No wonder there was no getting through to him. He was hooked, and, like so many gamblers, hoped for the big win which would retrieve his fortunes. The trouble was, he wasn't just taking himself down, he was taking her with him!

Though he wasn't aware of it, she had invested her own money in the business, so that there was very little

of her own inheritance left. She had never resented the
money, only the way it was being wasted. But this was
something else. Something far more serious, if she was
right and Daniel was hooked. He would need help, and
she didn't know if she was the one to give it. Even
supposing he would accept it. All she knew for certain
was that this was beyond her scope.

Descending the stairs on shaky legs, this time she
found the powder room with little trouble. The coolness of the peach-coloured room was a haven, to which
several other women had come to freshen up. Megan
moistened some pieces of paper towel and sat down at
one of the vanity mirrors, pressing the pads against her
warm cheeks. If she'd been the sort to give in to
hysteria, she would have been lying on her back
drumming her heels against the floor, she thought
wearily.

Her lashes dropped and she suddenly felt very tired.

'Finding Lucas too hot to handle?' a biting voice
challenged from beside her, and Megan blinked her
eyes open to find that the woman called Mona had
taken the next seat.

Lowering her hands, Megan tossed the paper into
the waste basket. She sensed trouble, and whilst she
knew that the sensible thing to do would be to get up
and leave she had never run from a fight. A quick
glance round proved that the room was empty now,
save for the two of them, so she didn't have to pull her
punches. Opening her bag, she took out a lipstick.

'Not at all. I've always been able to handle Lucas,'
she returned sweetly, setting the cat among the pigeons.

Mona turned on her chair to bring herself closer to
Megan. 'You'll never keep him. You don't have what
it takes!' she declared spitefully, and Megan felt her
hackles rise.

She produced a sultry smile. 'Strange, I've had no
complaints so far. Lucas seems more than satisfied,' she

rejoined. What utterly charming people Lucas knew! She had no conscience about defending a mythical romance from this unwarranted attack.

Mona's face lost any charm it might have had. 'Listen, you little tramp, I'm warning you to stay away from Lucas. Sonja is a friend of mine, and Lucas belongs to Sonja!'

Any number of people could have told Mona that she had just made a very bad mistake. Megan paled with anger. Nobody had ever called her a tramp before, and without any justification. Just who did the Monas and Sonjas of this world think they were that they could talk to her like that? Her chin lifted pugnaciously. If the woman wanted a fight, she could have one—in spades.

'Really? Does he know that? Lucas has always given the impression of belonging solely to himself.'

Tell-tale heat stole into the other woman's cheeks. She knew Megan was right, but refused to give way. 'You lured him on. There's no other way he would break a date with Sonja to go out with you. But mark my words. He might have you tonight, but that's all you're going to get!' Mona threatened nastily.

'Which is more than you'll ever have. You want him for yourself, don't you? But I bet he's never even looked at you, has he?' Megan made a wild guess, and knew she was right when the other woman turned pale.

'Bitch!' Mona snarled, and, with a flounce, rose to her feet and left the room.

Megan expelled an angry breath. That had been very unpleasant, though she was glad she had routed her enemy. The thought of Lucas with that woman made her shudder. Thank goodness he had better taste, although Sonja hadn't been much nicer. What did he see in them, or was that a naïve question? Her lips twisted. Probably. Not that it mattered; she wasn't interested in Lucas; she had just been defending herself.

She refused to listen to the tiny voice which said she had enjoyed squashing the woman too much to be totally disinterested. Taking a deep, calming breath, she slipped her lipstick back into her bag and made her way back to the nightclub.

She paused inside the doorway to get her bearings, but had no trouble picking out Lucas. She had the disconcerting feeling that she would always know exactly where he was, even in a crowded room. She began to make her way towards him, and that was when she realised he was talking to a woman seated at the next table. Her eyes narrowed. No, not just talking. From the way the woman was laughing, he was flirting with her quite outrageously. He couldn't be left alone for five minutes!

Anger made her quicken her step, until that tiny voice demanded to know what she was doing. What on earth was she getting angry about? She had no claim on Lucas, and didn't want one. What he did was none of her business. Her step faltered. It was a timely reminder, and a resigned smile curved her lips as she got her perspective back.

As if sensing her gaze, Lucas glanced round, his blue eyes meeting her mocking green ones. He must have read something in them, for his brows rose questioningly. I've just had a nasty exchange because of your roving eye, she thought, and here you are chatting up the nearest available woman!

She dropped her bag on the table and sat down. 'I'd be careful if I were you—the knives are out tonight,' she warned ironically, smiling coolly at the brunette, who was still hoping to regain Lucas's attention. The woman promptly turned her back.

Lucas's lips twitched. 'Been fighting, have you? I

wondered why you were gone so long,' he observed, his voice carrying a betraying wobble.

Megan picked up her drink, debated whether to throw it at him, and decided that drinking it would do her more good, even if it wouldn't be as much fun. 'I've just had a very interesting conversation with a friend of a friend of yours,' she informed him wryly.

Lucas stilled in the act of raising his glass to his lips. 'Ah. I detect Mona's heavy hand. You'd better tell me what happened.'

'I was warned off you, in no uncertain terms.' Megan smiled reminiscently, with all the friendliness of an angry tigress.

'I shouldn't imagine that went down too well,' Lucas surprised her by saying quite grimly.

Taking a sip of her drink, Megan pondered the fact that he actually sounded annoyed on her behalf. 'Like a lead weight,' she admitted ruefully.

'I'm sorry,' Lucas apologised, making her give him an odd look. 'You shouldn't have had to go through that. Mona took far too much upon herself.'

Well, well, well, Megan thought wonderingly, feeling better about the whole thing. She had never expected Lucas to champion her, but maybe she had done him an injustice. 'It doesn't matter. I got my own back.'

There was wry humour reflected in his blue eyes. 'I'm sure you did.'

Megan finally laughed. 'I was tempted to tell her you're no great catch!' she told him slyly.

'I'm surprised you didn't,' he remarked, sipping at his own drink and looking pleasantly relaxed.

Megan looked at him quite soberly. 'Frankly, she wouldn't have believed me. To people like Mona and Sonja you're the glittering prize. They'll have to learn the hard way that all that glistens isn't gold,' she sighed.

Lucas's laugh was harsh with cynicism. 'They don't

expect gold. So long as the diamonds are real they'll
have no regrets.'

Though she had vaguely guessed as much, she was
still shocked. 'That's the most mercenary thing I've
ever heard!'

Lucas shrugged dismissively. 'It happens to be true.
I'm a very wealthy man, with a reputation for being
generous when an affair is over. Women like Sonja see
an affair with me as an insurance policy against hard
times.'

Megan shuddered with distaste. 'If you know they
see you like that, how can you go out with them?'

'As a rule, I avoid the Sonjas of the world like the
plague. My relationships have always been with women
I like and respect, who know as well as I do that the
affair will last as long as it is mutually beneficial. I've
remained friends with them all.'

It sounded reasonable, but cold. Part of a different
world she was glad she didn't inhabit. 'Then why Sonja,
if she doesn't fit in?'

Much to her surprise, Lucas looked discomfited. 'She
was the flight attendant on the plane back from Hong
Kong last month. I needed a companion for a charity
do, and she was free that night. She was good fun, and
we went out a few times. When I knew I was coming
down here, she asked if I could give her a lift. Her
family live not far away. That was to be the end of it.'

Megan had to bite her lip to stop herself grinning.
He didn't sound at all happy with the way things had
turned out. Sonja wasn't the dumb blonde he'd
expected. She had claws and was intent on getting them
well into him. 'Something tells me Sonja has other
ideas!' she said cheerfully, and Lucas shot her a fulmi-
nating look.

'Think it's funny, do you?' he growled, then laughed
reluctantly. 'Unfortunately, you're right. I'm afraid
Sonja will have to go.'

'Do you think it will be that easy?' Megan asked, grinning all the more for he was allowing her to, at his expense.

'Probably not,' he admitted ruefully. 'There's bound to be a scene. Do you want to come and watch? No doubt you'd enjoy it.'

She pretended to think about it. 'I could render first aid. I have a badge.'

'And I know where you'd like to stick it!' he declared drily. 'On second thoughts, I'll go on my own.'

'Spoilsport!'

Grinning himself, Lucas drained his glass. 'I know you'd like to see blood, especially mine, but this time you'll be disappointed. Are you ready to go?'

She was. More than ready. It had been the strangest evening. Rather like an extended roller-coaster ride, all highs and lows. Lucas settled the bill, then they went to collect her shawl. As he draped it around her shoulders, Megan yawned.

'Sleepy?' Lucas asked, keeping his arm about her shoulders as he helped her down the steps and across to his car.

'A little, but I enjoyed myself tonight,' she confessed with the faintest hint of surprise.

Lucas picked it up. 'Even though you didn't expect to.'

'Well, you must admit it was chancy. All we ever do when we meet is fight,' Megan pointed out as he held the door open for her to climb in.

Lucas closed it after her and walked round to claim his own seat. 'Ever wondered why?' he probed, starting the engine.

She smiled faintly. 'Not particularly, though I suppose you have some wonderful theory,' she quipped easily.

'We fight, Red, because we like it,' Lucas countered smoothly, making her nerves twang. She had thought the same thing herself only the other day. 'What do you think that means?'

'That we're both masochists?' she ventured as they began to move and the darkness settled around them like a glove. The world shrank to the small space they sat in.

'It adds spice to our relationship,' Lucas corrected her, and Megan found her eyes drawn to where his hands rested on the steering wheel. They were long-fingered and capable as he manoeuvred the car with perfect control. They would have the same control as they roved over a woman's skin, bringing her to life. Bringing her pleasure.

She jerked straighter in her seat, alarmed at where her musings were taking her. Such thoughts were out of bounds. Especially when linked to Lucas. 'There's just one thing wrong with your theory—we don't have a relationship,' she pointed out coolly.

'Not yet,' he agreed, never taking his eyes from the road.

Megan felt her nerves jump. What did that mean? If he had the notion that she might somehow be available, she would put him straight at once. 'Not ever. I don't want a relationship with you.'

He laughed. 'I don't want one with you, either,' he said, and she wondered why his agreement didn't make her feel more secure.

They fell silent for the remainder of the journey. Though she tried not to be, she was very much aware of every move Lucas made. When his thigh muscles flexed she couldn't help wondering how his strength would feel against her softness. Her stomach lurched. Lord, she had to get a grip and stop fantasising like this about a man whose reputation with women made headline news. Even had she not had good reason not to get involved with anyone, she would never become Lucas's latest diversion.

When Lucas finally drew the car to a halt outside the house, she turned to him with a cool smile. 'Thank you for a lovely evening,' she said politely, and would have reached for the door release if Lucas hadn't swiftly leant across to stop her.

'It isn't quite over yet,' he told her softly, and her breath caught in her throat at his sudden closeness. It was impossible to see the colour of his eyes, but she could see them glittering.

The car seemed to be crackling with electricity, and her heart skipped several beats. 'What does that mean?'

'It means I think I ought to give you a little more information for your book,' he enlightened her silkily, his voice stroking over nerves never reached before.

Just when she needed them most, her wits seemed to go begging. 'Book?'

She sensed his smile. 'Mmm, you know. *Seduction— the Canfield Way*?' he prompted, using his free hand to brush a strand of hair off her cheek.

Megan jumped, regretting the whim which had made her tease him with that imaginary book. 'I think I've done enough research for tonight,' she argued far too breathlessly, and tried again to open the door, but Lucas wouldn't be budged. All she managed to do was bring herself so close to him that she could feel the brush of his breath on her cheek.

Her throat closed over and her lashes fluttered betrayingly. It was dark and they were alone. All she had to do was turn her head the merest fraction for their lips to touch. A tiny voice asked if it would really be so bad. Her sharply honed instinct for self-preservation said it could be catastrophic.

'I disagree. I think I should kiss you. Purely in the interests of science, of course,' he declared, and when she gasped and moved that fraction to look at him he brought his mouth down on hers.

Her first instinct was to fight him. She did raise one hand to push him away, but it remained clenched at his shoulder as sweet, hot sensations throbbed to life in the pit of her stomach and she found her will to fight draining out of every limb. Her mind went into a tailspin. As her defences crumbled with pitiful ease, he disarmed her with the tantalising brush of his lips over her own, inviting her participation with the soft stroke of his tongue.

Like a diver deprived too long of air, long-suppressed emotions battled through to the surface. All sense of danger was swamped beneath a wave of sensuality. She suddenly couldn't think, could only feel herself coming to life, and she craved that resurrection with a hunger which brought a moan to her throat as the teasing went on and on. Her head fell back, and there was no other option in the world for her than to part her lips and invite him to deepen the kiss.

With a growl of satisfaction his mouth opened on hers, his tongue gliding in to take possession, and her skin began to prickle with a white heat. It was as if she had been plugged into a circuit which gave her a positive charge of electricity. All she was conscious of was the stroking of his tongue on sensitive flesh and a compelling need to respond. She couldn't help herself. Her fingers skated up to his nape, finding the lush locks of hair, and clung on as her tongue duelled with his. Her eyes closed as her body melted against him, and her sighing moan filled the air.

At her capitulation, Lucas shifted, pulling her across him until she was cradled in his lap. Her whole body seemed to be pulsing, needing more, and she moved against him. Lucas groaned, and she felt his body surge against her, his arousal thickening her blood and sending it coursing through her veins. He drew her close, and the sensual exploration finally became a demand. Her senses swam and her free arm went around him, holding on as she responded with a wildness which, though it was a stranger to her, was so much a part of her nature. Uncaring, she flung herself willingly into the storm which raged around them.

As kiss followed kiss with breathtaking intensity, Lucas's hand traced a searing path down her back to the luscious curve of her hip, halting when it met the silky stretch of flesh below the hem of her dress, making her heart thud. Then slowly it began to rise again until it found the swell of her breast. Megan held her breath, then groaned as he took her into his palm and her nipple hardened into an aching point. It wasn't enough. She wanted him to touch her, and, as if he had read her mind, in the next instant he was pushing the tiny strap of her dress aside to ease the bodice away.

Yet instead of administering the touch she longed for Lucas tore his lips from hers and buried them against her neck with a groan.

Feeling deprived, Megan took a painful breath. 'Lucas?' she asked questioningly. Why had he stopped?

Lucas raised his head with a sigh. 'This is getting a little out of hand. If I don't stop, we'll end up making love in the car, and I haven't done that since I was a teenager!' he said wryly.

Sanity returned then, like an icy flood, taking the heat from her, leaving her cold with shock. Dear God, what had she been thinking of? Suddenly she was aware that she was still draped around him, and with a gasp of dismay she scrambled back to her own seat. Righting her dress, she had to swallow several times in order to be able to speak.

'That's nonsense. It wouldn't have gone that far!' she exclaimed thickly.

'Wouldn't it?' Lucas challenged huskily from the shadows of his own seat. 'I didn't want to stop, and, if you're honest, neither did you.'

Megan couldn't deny it. She hadn't wanted to stop.

Her body still ached with need, and she knew that if he touched her again now she wouldn't resist him. She was shocked by her uninhibited response, and her inability to control it. Control was her life.

She fought for it now, and achieved partial success, in that she was able to find something to say. 'Well, now I *know* I've done enough research for one night.'

Lucas laughed throatily. 'If there's any point you're not sure of, I can run over it again,' he offered, making heat rise in her once more.

She felt as if she'd been run over already. 'No, thanks; I've already got more than I bargained for.'

'I'll second that,' he retorted wryly. 'I think it's cold shower time for me. Not that I should be surprised. This was always on the cards.'

The rueful statement brought her head shooting round. 'What do you mean?'

Lucas shifted in his seat, the better to see her. 'There's no point in pretending it's not happening, Red. We've been aware of each other since the moment we met again.'

Her gasp was audible. She had known about herself, but, like a naïve idiot, she hadn't realised Lucas felt it too. And, having just gone to pieces in his arms, she'd look like an even bigger fool if she tried to deny it.

'It shouldn't be happening,' she insisted gruffly, her heart thudding sickeningly fast.

'Tell me about it!' Lucas exclaimed drolly, sounding much more normal. 'I got one hell of a shock when I realised I was strongly attracted to the girl who had taunted me unmercifully for more years than I cared to remember,' he went on huskily.

'Then why couldn't you just remember that and leave me alone?' she charged, knowing it was unfair to put the blame on him, but doing it to salve her pride.

Lucas shook his head. 'Because you set my heart thumping and my skin tingling. I'm a man, not a machine. I wanted you, Red. I still do. Every bit as much as you want me.'

Megan stared at him, knowing it was true. She'd never felt such a powerful need, and it made her tremble inside. But that only served to make her forgotten common sense reassert itself. She might want him, but she would not have him. She would make that very clear.

'Then you'll just have to want, because this is as far as it goes!' she declared tightly, and fumbled for the lock.

Lucas made no attempt to stop her this time. She clambered from the car, slammed the door and raced up the steps on legs which threatened to fail her. She prayed that Lucas would not follow her. She desperately needed to be alone to think. When she reached the sanctuary of her room, she dived inside like a rabbit into its hole and collapsed against the solid wood.

Oh, Lord, she was in trouble!

CHAPTER FIVE

MEGAN paced up and down her room, feeling distinctly edgy. It was late. Earlier she had showered in a vain attempt to relax, but she had merely ended up cleaner and no less restless. Nevertheless, she had slipped into the T-shirt she used to sleep in and climbed into bed— and lain awake for ages. In the end she had given up and taken to pacing instead.

What on earth had possessed her to respond to Lucas with such abandon? Being attracted wasn't new to her. She had subdued it successfully more than once, so why had the strength of purpose she valued so much gone begging tonight? She had fully intended to resist, but somehow she hadn't been able to. The second he had touched her she had become powerless, over-whelmed by an attraction so powerful that denial had been the last thing on her mind.

Reaching the end of the room, she leaned her forehead against the wall and groaned aloud. That was why she knew she was in trouble. She had never felt this pull with any of the other men she had been drawn to. She had believed herself to be in total control because she had been able to dismiss them. Now she knew better because the truth had jumped up and hit her. There was no comparison. She had found it easy to quell the stirrings of need because those men hadn't made her feel the way Lucas did.

With one kiss he had shown her how wrong she was. She hadn't wanted the others, but she did want Lucas. It was like an ache inside her. An emptiness which needed to be filled, but only by him. No other man would do. Her eyes closed, and she took a shaky breath.

The most terrifying thing, though, was realising she could have him, because Lucas wanted her too. His admission had shaken her and thrilled her at the same time. The knowledge that the feeling was mutual made her tremble inside even now. Swallowing hard, she began to retrace her uneasy steps.

For the first time in her life she was truly being faced with temptation, and part of her longed to give in. Lucas was dangerously alluring, his pull strong. She had lost herself in his arms tonight, forgetting everything. Nothing had seemed to matter, save that the wonderful things she was feeling should go on. And they could, if she were to have an affair with him. He was used to women finding him attractive, used to exploring mutual feelings. He probably thought she was too. But she wasn't.

Finding herself level with the window-seat, she sank down onto the cushions, more anxious than she could remember feeling for a long time. Tonight had brought her into direct conflict with her own rules. That was partly the cause of her restlessness—for the first time since university she was being tempted to break them. Lucas took her to places nobody else had, and she knew that if she showed him the slightest encouragement he would follow up what had happened tonight. And whilst a wanton part of her was inclined to do just that, the saner part urged caution.

Was it worth destroying her hard-won peace of mind for the fleeting benefits of sexual satisfaction? No sooner had the question entered her mind than the answer followed it. No, it wasn't.

The tension drained out of her as sanity returned. The chill of reality made her shiver. Finding herself susceptible to Lucas's potent maleness had opened her eyes. She had discovered she was not the person she had thought herself to be, but nothing else had changed. Sex was not the answer. Experience had

taught her that, and so she must fight this unexpected
attraction, and conquer it.

She knew that facing Lucas again wouldn't be easy.
She couldn't pretend that nothing had happened, but
she could make good and sure it didn't happen again.
She would keep her distance from now on, and Lucas
would get the message. She was not available as a
diversion.

As it turned out, it was two days before she saw Lucas
again, because he was called away on business. Cow-
ardly though it was, she welcomed the respite. Not so
welcome was the fact that Daniel had become even
more elusive, so she'd had no chance to speak to him
either.

That was how matters stood as Megan drove back to
Terrell's after a depressing meeting with their bank
manager. She had the car windows down, allowing the
warm air to rush in at her. Daniel should have gone,
and his absence hadn't pleased the manager, but as
Daniel hadn't come home last night, as usual, the job
had been left to her. She hadn't been in a conciliatory
mood herself, having overslept, yet somehow she had
managed to persuade the man to extend their
overdraft.

A small victory, but it had improved her mood as
she'd returned to her car. Shrugging off the jacket of
her trouser suit, she had tossed it onto the back seat
and rolled up the sleeves of her silk blouse, before
setting off on the return journey.

It was a beautiful day, with enough breeze to make
it perfect sailing weather. To her left she could see a
lone sailor out on the river, and envied him his freedom. She couldn't remember the last time she had
been able to just take off. A mile further, and with a
twist of the road, she got a better view, and her lips
parted in surprise. Closer, she recognised the craft as

Daniel's dinghy, and although he was tacking away from her she knew he must be bringing her in to the tiny landing at the head of the creek.

She didn't stop to marvel that he was actually around at this time of day. This was a gift horse she wasn't going to look in the mouth. She needed to talk to him, and there might not be a better time. Pressing her foot down, she raced to get to the tiny beach before him.

Daniel's car wasn't in the yard when she parked there, but then he had probably sailed down from the house. Ignoring the shed where Ted would already be hard at work, she cut off along the path through the trees which led to the beach. From the sound of whistling, she knew he had got there ahead of her. At least he sounded as if he was in a good mood, and she hoped that was a promising sign.

However, as she rounded the last bend in the path, and the trees opened onto grass leading down to a sandy beach with a small landing-stage, one glance was enough to reveal not Daniel but Lucas. He must have returned whilst she was in town.

He hadn't heard her arrive, which was just as well, for seeing him so suddenly like this had taken her breath away. In jeans, with the checked shirt he must have started out wearing tied around his waist by the sleeves, his hair mussed and his cheeks flushed, Lucas looked vitally alive. Busy with the sail, he moved with instinctive male grace, exuding power and confidence. The tanned flesh of his back rippled as he worked, and to Megan he looked barely tamed, as free-spirited as the flapping canvas, always threatening to break free. Something hit her below the ribs with the force of a blow, and she found herself watching in helpless fascination.

A feeling of vulnerability assailed her, because, heaven help her, he called to her. He called to her in a way no other man ever had. She was compelled to admit to herself that looking at him gave her immense pleasure, and in doing so experienced again that wild stirring of the blood. Her throat ached. How could one man make her feel so incredibly alive that he tempted her to break all her own rules?

She didn't know how, she only knew he did, and that made him all the more dangerous. Even now a wayward part of her was urging her to go forward, but she resisted, knowing that it only confirmed her need to keep her distance. Though it seemed to take an effort, she turned to go.

'See anything you liked?' Lucas's silky question floated over the air to her, making her jerk round again.

Colour washed in and out of her cheeks as she realised he had known she was there all the time. Unable to retreat now, she took a couple of steps towards him. Had she seen anything she liked? Dear heaven, she had liked everything far too much! 'I thought you were Daniel,' she pointed out defensively.

Lucas's head finally turned towards her, and he eyed her with a faint smile lingering around his lips. 'For about five seconds. But don't worry. I don't mind you looking. I enjoy looking at you, too. You're very easy on the eye,' he responded softly, and her stomach lurched at the easy compliment. She shouldn't have liked it, but her senses were refusing to cooperate with her brain. Whenever she came within feet of Lucas she stopped being a thinking human being and became a seething mass of emotions.

She watched him finish what he was doing and step onto the landing-stage. Her throat tightened. He looked too damned alluring, and she wished he would put his shirt on and shut temptation away. However, he showed no intention of doing so, and Megan decided it was time to make her position quite clear.

'Stop it, Lucas. I'm not interested,' she ordered shortly, and he flashed her a knowing look.

'You were interested the other night,' he observed, setting her nerves twanging as vivid memories assailed her. Having made sure the craft was secured, he walked towards her.

Lord, how she wished that night had never happened; then she wouldn't be trying to defend an indefensible position. 'Don't play games with me. I'm not in the mood,' she returned quellingly, trying to make it sound as if she meant it, but to her own ears merely sounding petulant.

It didn't work, anyway. Lucas ran his tingling blue gaze over her and inclined his head enticingly. 'I know a sure-fire way of getting you in the mood. Want to try it?' he invited, moving another step closer.

Megan had expected him to tease her, but he was being deliberately provocative, and with sudden insight she knew he had been expecting her. Maybe not here and now, but sometime. He had known she would come to deny anything and everything, and he wasn't going to let her. The other night she had aroused the hunter, and unless she could persuade him he was following the wrong scent he would use all his skills to trap her. It didn't help that she was hampered by her own wanton senses, but it made her more determined to win.

'No, I do not want to try it!' she exclaimed tautly. 'You're being ridiculous. Remember all the reasons why this shouldn't be happening.'

His brows rose mockingly. 'Is that what you did? Is it working?'

That hit her confidence at its weakest spot. Because, no matter how she tried, reminding herself of the distance her rules demanded, it wasn't working. Unable to hold his gaze, her eyes dropped, and he laughed huskily. Realising what she had given away, Megan abruptly put some distance between them, needing the breathing space. 'I told you the other night that that was the end of it,' she pointed out unevenly.

Lucas took his weight on one leg and eyed her averted face consideringly. 'Look me in the eye and say that.'

Taunted, Megan swung to face him, her lips parted to snap out the words, but he was far closer than she expected, and her throat closed over, making it impossible for her to get the words out. Instead she found herself staring at him helplessly whilst her senses rioted in response to his nearness. Lucas could have said anything then, but to her amazement his lips twisted into a wry smile.

'I know the feeling,' he admitted huskily, holding her eyes, and she knew he was as disconcerted by this unexpected attraction as she was. However, it was clear that he was willing to go with it. To test it and see where it would take him. 'Strange the way things turn out,' he remarked, walking around her to lean against the nearest tree.

Megan shifted to face him, feeling unreal. In a way she envied him his ease with his own sexuality, but it didn't alter the fact that she could not allow herself the same luxury. There were good reasons for her not to get involved with him, or anyone, and they hadn't changed.

'There's nothing here for you, Lucas,' she asserted as strongly as she could.

'Let me be the judge of that,' he countered softly, and colour rose in her cheeks as his intense blue eyes began a lazy inspection of her from head to toe. His gaze was a caress, designed to get a reaction, and her body responded without her volition. Megan felt her nipples tighten into hard buds, and knew they were pressing blatantly against her silk shirt. She didn't dare cross her arms as she was tempted to, for then he would know exactly what reaction he was getting.

Yet when his eyes finally met hers again it was obvious that he knew. 'I dreamt about you these last few nights,' he informed her in a husky drawl which touched her nerves and set them tingling.

She knew she had given him ample cause to think she might be willing to be seduced, which meant that she was fighting an uphill battle, but she couldn't stop until she had made him accept that she meant what she said. So far all she had done was undermine herself. She had to get a grip and fight this unwanted attraction to the last breath. It would help if he put his shirt on, but the mere mention of it would be more ammunition to him. She would have to try and ignore that broad expanse of male flesh.

'Nightmares can be scary,' she sympathised, with a flash of her old spirit, and he smiled in a way which set her heart tripping.

'Would you have comforted me, Red?' he taunted, and she shivered when his eyes dropped to her lips and remained there, so that it almost felt as if he was touching her. Her palms went damp as she acknowledged that he was good at this. Slowly but surely, curling tendrils of electric awareness were wreathing the air between them, with nothing more than a look.

Stiffening her resolve, she made herself remember that he was good because he had had plenty of practice. She was just another in a long, long line. 'I would have thrown cold water over you and let you fend for yourself!' she retorted, and he threw back his head and laughed.

Which didn't help her at all, because she liked the sound of it far too much. Plus he looked so carefree, she was tempted to join him! Lord, this was crazy!

'I find arguing with you strangely addictive,' he declared when he had sobered again.

Megan wanted to groan out loud. This was not what she wanted to hear. Instead of warning him off, everything she said was being used against her. 'Lucas, be sensible!' she implored again, but he shook his head.

'There's a time and place to be sensible, and this isn't it. We're attracted to each other.'

She swallowed painfully, unable to deny it. 'I don't want this.'

His smile was softly derisive. 'Do you think we have much choice?'

Megan caught her breath. He made it sound... ordained. As if the gods had spoken and there was nothing they could do. She shivered, shutting her mind against that primeval part of her which recognised his statement. 'Of course we have a choice. We can simply turn our backs on it and pretend it never happened!'

Lucas pushed himself away from the tree and prowled towards her with leonine intent. Megan backed away instinctively, unfortunately coming up against another tree which blocked her retreat. Abruptly she found herself with nowhere to go. All she could do was wait as he came to stand in front of her. His hand reached out, and she breathed in sharply as with one finger he traced the fullness of her bottom lip.

'Can you? Because I don't think I can. Like I said, I didn't sleep very well last night,' he said huskily.

Megan felt that touch in every part of her. It was as if by it he had taken total possession. She could no more run than a one-day-old chick could fly. More, she wanted to slip the tip of her tongue between her lips and taste him, and that shocked her because it meant that with a few kisses he had unlocked a wealth of sensuality which she hadn't realised she possessed. Certainly her one brief affair hadn't stirred her this much. Nobody had ever tempted her the way Lucas did. Nobody had ever driven her mindless with the passionate longing of his kiss.

There was all that and more right here, right now, and she felt she was caught in quicksand, struggling hopelessly to be free. She didn't know how to fight it, knew only that she must, and that gave her enough strength to twist her head to one side and force his hand to fall away. It was a small success and she hurried to bolster it.

'Perhaps you should have given Sonja a ring,' she retorted shakily, but only managed to draw a laugh.

'I'm afraid Sonja wouldn't do. You see, all I could think about was the sweetness of your lips.'

Her throat closed over as his words conjured up the moment in vivid colour. 'It was just a kiss, Lucas, nothing special,' she denied thickly, licking her lips and inadvertently getting the taste of him she had wanted only seconds before.

His eyes followed the movement, and he groaned softly. 'If that's so, then you won't mind kissing me again just to make sure, will you?' he challenged, moving to prop his hands against the tree at either side of her head, effectively trapping her.

Megan immediately found it incredibly hard to breathe. She wanted to push herself free, but knew she dared not touch him for fear that her hands would betray her as they had that night. 'Damn you, Lucas, let me go or I'll hit you!' she cried in desperation.

'That isn't what you really want to do,' he declared softly, taking her breath away. 'Deny it as much as you like, but we both know something special happened that night, and I've been waiting ever since to kiss you and make it all happen again.'

She was floundering and she knew it. 'You're wrong. Nothing happened and nothing will,' she asserted in a hopeless attempt to freeze him off. 'Carry on with this and you'll only make me despise you.'

'A lot of sour words pass through those lovely lips of

yours, Red, but I know now they taste like nectar. It's something I could very easily become addicted to.'

Dear Lord, why was it that everything he said had the power to set her nerves jangling? How was it possible for one man to turn her world upside down in so short a time? 'This is crazy!' she declared faintly.

Lucas's smile faded, banked fire reflected in his eyes. 'The other night you turned to flame in my arms.'

The husky sound of his voice was sending tremors up and down her spine, weakening her knees and her resistance. She knew she had to do something to break free, otherwise she might do something else far worse. 'That was a mistake,' she insisted thickly, and he smiled slowly.

'A statement like that can't be allowed to pass, so let's put it to the test, shall we?' he suggested, and closed the gap between them.

'No, Lucas!' she protested desperately, bringing her hands up to push him away, but he caught them easily and forced them back against the tree.

'Megan, yes!' he countered with a husky growl, lowering his head.

Caught between the muscular planes of his body and the tree, there was nowhere for Megan to retreat to, and she groaned helplessly in her throat as his mouth found hers. She tried to resist the soft touch of his kiss, the sensual glide of his tongue along her closed lips, but even so small a contact started a conflagration inside her. Heat curled upwards, setting her nerves sizzling. When she wanted to be strong, her muscles seemed to weaken, turning traitor to her mind.

Then his mouth left hers, trailing along her jaw to her ear, making her shiver as his tongue traced the sensitive skin before foraying down to where her pulse beat frantically in her throat. She uttered a stifled gasp as his tongue stroked the spot, and bit her lip as his lips lowered to the open V of her blouse. Her breasts tightened, her nipples hardening to aching points which so craved his touch that when, in the next instant, his lips found one peak through the silk blouse, she couldn't stop her body arching into him.

She gasped again, and with a growl of triumph his head rose and his mouth found hers again. She had always been lost, she realised, right from the very beginning, and now there was no thought of fight in her. Her lips parted to the insistent pressure of his tongue, and when her own tongue melded with his he released her hands and slid his arms round her, drawing her tight to his strongly aroused body.

The knowledge that he wanted her was dizzying, sending all thought of self-preservation to the four winds. There was only now, and the feel of his hands and lips on her. Her own arms were around his neck, her small hands sliding into his hair and clinging on tightly. Lucas groaned and she shivered as one large hand pulled her blouse free and slipped underneath to run up and down her velvety skin.

When he lowered her to the grass, she didn't resist but welcomed the weight of him. His kiss deepened, becoming more and more demanding, and she returned it hungrily, a willing victim of her own need. The rights and wrongs of what she was doing were light years from her mind.

Beneath her blouse, his hand found the front fastening of her bra and released it, pushing it aside to fasten on the jutting mound of her breast, and Megan cried out at the intense pleasure which swept down through her body to increase the throbbing ache deep inside her. His thumb flicked back and forth, circling and teasing until pleasure was almost pain.

Lucas lifted his head then, and she opened dazed eyes to stare up at him. 'Sweet heaven, what you do to me! I want you, Megan. I've never wanted any woman as much as I want you right now!' he growled, and her heart lurched.

Had he not spoken, she doubted that she would have come to her senses, but he had and his words were like a douche of cold water. She froze, her heart thudding wildly as she dragged in air. It wasn't true. He wanted her the same he wanted those other women, he just used the words to get what he wanted. Well, he wasn't going to get her!

Lucas felt her stillness and his eyes searched her face. 'What is it?'

Green eyes clouded with anger met his. 'Let me up,' she ordered coldly.

For a second he looked as if he was going to argue, then with a sigh he rolled away and sat up. Free to move, Megan scrambled to her feet, her legs about as useful as those of a newborn foal. She refused to look at him as she righted her clothes with more haste than accuracy. She knew that she had just had a narrow escape, no thanks to herself. If he hadn't mentioned those wretched women...! She ground her teeth in self-disgust.

Lucas was on his feet too, watching her curiously. 'What happened? You were with me up to that point,' he declared, sounding so cool and in control that she wanted to slap him. What other proof did she need that this was nothing out of the ordinary for him?

Megan glared at him. 'It was getting a little crowded down there!' she snapped, nodding towards the flattened area. As she saw him frown, her lip curled. 'With you, me and all your other women!' she enlightened him, only to see amusement curve his far too attractive mouth.

'Jealous, Red? I'll remember that for next time,' he had the gall to say, and she fumed.

'There will be no next time, and I most certainly was not jealous!'

His eyebrows rose. 'Then why are you so angry?' he asked softly, neatly taking the wind out of her sails.

Why *was* she angry? It was nothing to her who he had gone out with. He meant nothing to her. Nothing. Yet the reminder of the existence of those women hurt, a small voice taunted her. Only because he was attempting to add her to the list, she argued, and set her jaw. 'If I'm angry, then it's because I didn't appreciate being given that old line!' she shot back.

To her annoyance, Lucas refused to react the way she wanted him to. Instead of looking shamefaced, he had the nerve to look serious. 'It wasn't a line, Red. I meant it. The truth is I've never felt like this before.'

Despite herself her throat closed over. 'You can't really expect me to believe that?' she challenged with a shaky laugh.

Lucas dragged his hands through his hair, unwittingly drawing her eyes to his chest. She had to swallow hard and look away. 'The most I expect from you is a fight, but I don't mind that. Deny it all you like, but what we have here is a pretty powerful combination. I'm not going to walk away from it, or allow you to.'

Her heart lurched. 'Is that a threat?'

His expression softened to somewhere between sensuality and tenderness. 'No, it's a promise.'

For a moment all she could do was look at him as she turned to jelly inside, then from somewhere she found the spunk to stiffen her spine. 'I won't sleep with you.'

'Maybe I want more,' he suggested.

Megan shook her head. 'I won't have an affair with you either,' she declared as firmly as she could, considering he was turning her inside out.

'Why not? It would be good between us.'

She knew it, but it was not a good enough reason to abandon the rules she lived by. 'It's still no.'

'I'm not going to give up trying to persuade you to

change your mind,' Lucas returned, and she smiled grimly.

'I never thought you would. I can't stop you, but you'll be wasting your time.'

'Time will tell,' he said irritatingly, and finally untied the shirt from his waist and slipped it on. Catching sight of her fiery eyes, he traced a finger down her cheek. 'OK, Red, if I can't interest you in an affair, how about coming out with me this afternoon?'

The gentle touch and the change of subject threw her. She didn't know what to make of him. He seemed to be able to turn his emotions on and off at will. One minute he was trying to persuade her into bed, the next he was inviting her out as if nothing had happened.

She blinked at him. 'In the boat?'

His look grew wry. 'I don't think so. What you and I need is company, not finding ourselves alone in a tiny boat,' he said mockingly, and she realised then that he was just as churned up as she was; he just managed to hide it better. Strangely enough, that comforted her.

She took a steadying breath. 'What were you doing with the dinghy anyway?'

'Dan gave me the use of it, and as it was a perfect morning for being on the water I decided to sail down instead of using the car,' he explained.

'To ask me to go out with you, I suppose?' she asked unsteadily, and jumped when he took her chin in his hand.

Lucas stared down broodingly into her startled eyes. 'That was my intention, until we got sidetracked. I had this urge to be with you, and I didn't want to give you any more time to think. I want your company, Red, so what do you say?'

He was twisting her in knots. His touch was gentle, and he sounded sincere. She was tempted. She knew she was supposed to be keeping her distance, but would it really hurt to go with him? Wouldn't it do her good to get away from the problems which surrounded her for a while? Her conscience told her these were all just excuses, but somehow she couldn't make herself listen. She wasn't going to go mad. She wasn't going to kick over the traces. She was simply contemplating spending the afternoon with an attractive man who wanted her company.

Because you want to be with him, no matter what, an inner voice informed her, and she ignored that too. One afternoon wasn't going to compromise her.

Easing back a step, so that his hand fell away, she cleared her throat. 'Where would we go?'

Lucas took a deep breath before answering, as if her reply had been important to him. 'Some friends of mine moved down here six months ago. They've invited me over for the afternoon.'

'They wouldn't be expecting me,' she pointed out, and he pulled a wry face.

'No, but, like you, they'd expect me to turn up with someone. Peggy nags me about it all the time. She wants me to settle down and raise a family of my own.'

'You, with children? I don't believe it,' Megan scoffed lightly. But she did believe it. She had a vivid mental picture of him with blue-eyed, dark-haired children, and she envied him. Envied him so much it was as if a vice had clamped about her heart.

Lucas tutted. 'It may not be your ideal, but I'd like to have half a dozen.'

Megan found emotion suddenly welling into her throat, and had to swallow hard to shift it. Because the subject hurt, she made light of it. 'Six? Wouldn't your wife have anything to say about it?'

'OK, I'll amend that to at least two. I know what it's like to be an only child, and, while it has certain advantages, it really isn't much fun.'

Megan cast him a frowning glance. 'You were lonely?' she asked. Somehow she had always had the

idea that Lucas was perfectly happy in his self-sufficient
way.

He sent her a teasing look. 'Feeling sorry for me,
Red?'

She tipped her chin at him. 'And if I am?'

'Join me this afternoon. You can't do anything about
my childhood, but you can brighten up my afternoon.'

A curling tendril of warmth sprang to life in her
stomach at the idea that she could do anything as
special as brighten his day. It wasn't true, and it only
showed how dangerous Lucas was that part of her
actually wanted to believe it nevertheless. It went some
way to filling the huge emptiness inside her. Which was
frightening. She had learned to live with the hole by
ignoring it. Now, suddenly, she was very much aware
of it, and of a yearning need to fill it.

And that brought her up short, because there was
nothing she could fill it with, and she didn't want to
remember the pain. Dismayed to find herself thinking
of things that she had hoped were long buried, Megan
shivered. To spend the afternoon with him would be
sheer folly.

'Sorry, but I've got too much to do,' she refused
shortly, heading for the path back to the yard.

Frowning, Lucas fell in step beside her. 'Doing what,
precisely? Have you suddenly been inundated with
requests for yacht designs?' he challenged, shooting her
down so swiftly that she winced and sent him a daggers
look even as she kept on walking.

'Thanks, I needed reminding!'

Lucas sighed, catching her arm to halt her in her
tracks. 'You'll weather it, Red. You're too good to go
under,' he declared, and his confidence in her brought
a flush to her cheeks.

'Maybe you could try telling that to Daniel,' she said
wryly, and Lucas frowned.

'I thought the problem was just the recession,' he

said, making her sharply aware that she had almost said too much.

'Oh, it is,' she confirmed with a laugh, but Lucas didn't smile.

'I've noticed he doesn't seem to be around much.'

Megan caught her breath. 'Yes, well, there isn't an awful lot for him to do.' As ever she made excuses for her brother, though she knew he wouldn't appreciate them.

It was Lucas who started them walking again. 'You know, you could get a job with any of the top companies on the strength of your work. You don't have to rely on Terrell's. I'm acquainted with several of the executives personally and would be glad to put in a word for you.'

She was truly lost for words for a moment, because it was a very generous offer. She was beginning to realise there was a great deal more to Lucas Canfield than she had suspected. Her voice, when she spoke, was gruff. 'Thanks, but Terrell's is my home. I. . .' Need it, she had been about to reveal, then changed her mind. 'I couldn't leave it.'

Lucas nodded. 'I can understand that, just as I can see the worry is wearing you down. You need a break, Megan.'

She couldn't help but smile drily. 'You're saying your offer is purely altruistic?' she queried, and he laughed ruefully.

'No, but if I promise to keep my hands to myself will you come?' he argued persuasively, making her hesitate.

She knew she shouldn't. Lucas was dangerous, and she was far too susceptible, and yet. . .'Well. . .'

'Come on, Red, you know you want to,' he urged as they emerged from the trees into the sunlight.

She turned her face up to it, realising she hadn't seen

more than the inside of the office for weeks. Lord knew he was right, and she needed the break, so why not?

'All right, I'll come,' she said swiftly, before she could change her mind, and hoped she wouldn't live to regret it.

Lucas glanced at his watch. 'Fine. I've got to sail the boat back before the tide changes, so why don't you drive back to the house and change into something more summery? I'll meet you back there as soon as I can, OK?'

'What about lunch?' she asked. She had skipped breakfast because of the appointment, and was already feeling the pangs of hunger. Lucas waved that away.

'That's taken care of. Jack's manning the barbecue. They'll be expecting us about half past one,' he declared, and with a wave of his hand he set off back the way they had come.

Megan stared after him, worrying at her lip, wondering if she was being wise. She couldn't remember ever feeling this churned up inside. So embattled by the conflicting emotions inside her. Probably because there had never been any conflict before Lucas. She had no experience to go on; all she could seem to do was stagger from one emotional upheaval to another, hoping to survive intact. Maybe putting herself in the way of another upset wasn't the wisest thing she had ever done, but it was too late now. Whatever happened, she would have to live with it.

CHAPTER SIX

JACK and Peggy Laker lived in a thatched cottage which had roses climbing the walls and was surrounded by a sprawling cottage garden awash with colour and scents. Peggy, a pretty woman in her late twenties, came to meet them as they drove up. Lucas waved to her as he came round to help Megan out of the car.

'What have you done with them, Peg? Tied them to a tree somewhere?' he asked, grinning, and the woman laughed.

'What, and spoil their treat? I haven't been able to keep them still since they heard you were coming.' A yell split the air just then, and Peggy rolled her eyes. 'Here come the little darlings now,' she said, with despairing fondness.

Megan, as amused as she was confused, turned in time to see two miniature tornadoes tear round the side of the cottage and hurtle themselves at Lucas. He fielded them with a roar, swinging them up and round to cries of 'Uncle Lucas! Uncle Lucas!'

Transfixed, Megan watched as the five-year-old twin boys gripped Lucas around the neck with unbridled affection. An affection which was fully returned, judging by the grin on his face. He looked so right with them, so natural, she thought.

'He'll make a wonderful father,' Peggy observed from beside her, glancing speculatively from Megan to Lucas and back.

Megan found that her throat had become so tight, it was hard to speak. 'He adores them,' she said huskily.

'They adore him,' Peggy added softly, watching as Lucas lowered her sons to the ground and allowed himself to be dragged off. He cast an apologetic grin over his shoulder as he went. 'They'll be all over him, and he'll love every minute of it. Sometimes I think he's just a big kid himself. By the way, in case you hadn't realised, I'm Peggy. The terrors are Martin and Michael. And you must be Megan. Lucas has told us all about you.'

'He has?' Megan exclaimed in surprise.

Peggy quickly slipped her arm through Megan's and urged her to follow the path Lucas and the boys had taken. 'Don't worry, it was nothing bad. He's very fond of you, you know. You're as lovely as he said you were, and I don't doubt just as wonderfully talented. You design boats, I'm told. I'm hopeless at drawing myself, but Lucas says your designs are amongst the best he's seen.'

'High praise indeed,' Megan murmured drily, whilst inside she felt warmth spreading through her at the idea of Lucas speaking well of her to his friends. However, what brought colour to her cheeks was the uneasy feeling that Peggy was putting a vastly different interpretation on her being here with Lucas, and she hastened to put her right. 'He always did give credit where it was due, but it's not personal.'

'Hmm, that's exactly what he said too,' Peggy remarked with amused satisfaction. 'Now, let's see what mischief they've got up to, and I'll introduce you to Jack at the same time.'

Megan allowed herself to be led off, knowing that Peggy had only been more convinced by the denial that there was anything between herself and Lucas. She wondered what the woman would say if she explained that all Lucas wanted to do was get her into bed. Not that she would say anything of the sort. Let Peggy imagine what she liked; she would have to change her mind when nothing came of it.

Her husband, Jack, turned out to be a man of Lucas's

age, stockier, with rounded features and a jolly personality. He took his attention from the barbecue to greet Megan warmly and press a glass of something deliciously fruity into her hand.

'I hope you're hungry. Peg has laid on enough food to feed a small army,' he teased his wife, who poked her tongue out at him then excused herself to go and prepare the salads.

Having had her offer of help refused, Megan found her eyes drawn irresistibly to where Lucas was engaging in a rowdy game of football with the irrepressibly giggling twins. A smile curled the corners of her lips.

Following her gaze, Jack grinned. 'You like children, Megan?'

Painful fingers tightened about her heart, but her voice was soft. 'Oh, yes.' There had been a brief time when she couldn't stand the pain of being with her friends and their families, but that had passed. Now, although there were some things she still would not do, she took pleasure in watching the children grow, closing off her mind to her own emptiness.

'Good,' Jack pronounced, turning back to his sausages. 'Lucas is crazy about them.'

Megan caught her breath as once again she got the unspoken message that the friendly couple thought she and Lucas were an item. What on earth had Lucas been saying to give them that impression? As soon as she could she would ask him, and get him to put the record straight. For now all she could do was shrug off the friendly teasing.

'Have you known Lucas long?' she asked, sipping at the refreshing drink.

'Since university, although I've only been working for him for five years. We used to live in London, but neither of us wanted to raise the children there. We didn't think we could do anything about it, though, because I didn't want to leave the company. It was

Lucas who came up with the ideal solution. He suggested I work from home, and. . .here we are. It's all worked out perfectly,' Jack informed her as he removed the cooked food from the griddle and refilled it.

Her eyebrows rose. Not many employers would be so thoughtful, even for friends. 'He must be unique.'

Jack wiped his hands on the apron he was wearing and came to join her. 'He is that. To look at him now, you'd never guess he was the head of a multi-million-dollar company, would you?'

As if to illustrate the claim, Lucas collapsed onto the lawn and the boys piled on top of him. Megan laughed as they bounced and he groaned. Then the strangest thing happened. It was as if the earth shifted under her feet, as in her mind she saw the same picture with different players. Lucas was there, and the boys, but she was there too. They were a family, and there was so much happiness in the shared laughter, she could scarcely breathe.

Her heart lurched, and the scene vanished, leaving behind a sense of loss so sharp that she wanted to cry out. Pain seemed to fill every part of her, and her fingers tightened around her glass so tightly that the slender shaft snapped, cutting into her palm. With a gasp of shock she stared at the welling blood as the pieces of glass dropped to shatter on the patio with the noise of a thunderclap.

'Don't move,' Jack ordered as he grabbed up a napkin from the table and pressed it to the wound.

'I'm so sorry,' Megan apologised thickly, feeling colour come and go in her cheeks. Nothing like that had ever happened to her before.

'It was just an accident,' Jack said easily, moving her away from the slivers of glass at her feet as Lucas and the boys rushed up.

'What happened?' Lucas's sharp question made her glance up to find him frowning down at her in concern.

'Her glass broke,' his friend answered for her. Seeing his sons hovering anxiously in the background, he smiled at them reassuringly. 'Go and ask Mummy for the dustpan and brush, boys.'

Lucas took her hand from Jack's. 'I'll see to this. You'd better stay and make sure the food doesn't end up as a casualty too,' he said tersely, already steering Megan towards the house.

'Is she going to faint?' Michael wanted to know, walking beside them as his brother ran on ahead.

'I hope not,' Megan answered raggedly, feeling rather light-headed.

'Your face went all funny,' he went on seriously. 'Mummy faints when she cuts herself.'

'Poor Mummy.'

Michael shrugged. 'She's OK when Daddy kisses her better. Are you going to kiss her better, Uncle Lucas?'

Megan's heart leapt into her throat and she glanced up into Lucas's amused blue eyes. 'Do you think I should?' he asked the boy without looking away.

'Yeah,' Martin declared firmly. 'Mummy likes being kissed.'

'That settles it, then,' Lucas murmured, and opened the door to the downstairs cloakroom. Megan found herself hustled inside and made to sit on the toilet seat. Seconds later Peggy arrived.

'First-aid box,' she said, handing it over, and Lucas balanced it on the cistern. 'Go and help Daddy, Michael. Tell him I'll be there in a minute. Don't touch anything, and don't run off!' she called to his retreating back. 'How is it?'

'Fortunately it hasn't gone too deep. A plaster should do it,' Lucas assured her, holding Megan's hand under the cold-water tap.

'Thank goodness. I'll leave her in your capable

hands, then,' Peggy decided, and gave Megan a sympathetic smile before vanishing.

Megan winced as he probed the cut for any fragments of glass. 'I feel like a sideshow at the circus!' she exclaimed fretfully.

'What do you expect if you will go in for these sort of dramatics?' Lucas challenged gruffly. 'How did you manage to do it?'

I had a vision of myself as part of a family, and the sky fell in, she said silently. 'I don't know.'

'Well, you were lucky you didn't do any serious damage. You'll live, though I don't think my heart can take too many shocks like that. You looked as if you'd been mortally wounded.'

It had felt as if she had. She had thought herself long past such emotional reactions, but that had been as sharp as in the early days. 'I didn't mean to shock you.'

Lucas studied the job he had done bandaging the wound. 'In future consider my constitution and check with me before you take up anything dangerous like knife-juggling, OK?' he ordered wryly, and she smiled faintly.

'You never used to be so worried about me. I was just a pest.'

'You're still a pest, Red. However, sometimes things change and take us by surprise. How's that?'

Now that the shock had worn off, Megan was very much aware of their closeness in the tiny room. 'Much better, thanks.'

'Now all I have to do is kiss you better,' Lucas pronounced softly, and when she automatically looked up he swiftly took her lips in a kiss that was as shattering as it was brief. It was so tender, it brought a lump to her throat, then he drew back, holding her gaze. 'Better?'

'Better' didn't come nearly close to describing her feelings. She cleared her throat, vaguely aware that she should break the spell which held them, but finding it strangely impossible. 'You're supposed to kiss the wound, not me.'

He half smiled, right down into her soul. 'Does that mean you didn't like it?'

Oh, she'd liked it all right. Far too much for safety. Her lips tingled, wanting more. This was getting out of hand. She had to put a stop to it before she closed the space between them, as every nerve she possessed was urging her to do.

Swallowing hard, she dragged her gaze free. 'I think we should go and join the others now.'

'You're right. This is neither the time nor the place,' Lucas agreed huskily, stepping back.

The small space this created between them allowed her brain to start working again. 'There will never be a right time or place.'

'There will be, and when we find it you won't be running away, Red,' he stated with such conviction that she shivered.

She said nothing, knowing words would not do. She would have to show him by her actions how wrong he was. Turning away, she walked back outside to where the others waited for them, Lucas a step behind her.

'We were about to send out a search party!' Jack called, and Megan was once more uncomfortably aware that both husband and wife were watching them with unfeigned speculation.

'What have you been saying to them?' she hissed at him as they crossed to the picnic table the boys already occupied. 'They think we're a couple!'

'We are,' Lucas observed calmly.

'Not in the way they mean! You must have said something.'

Lucas sighed. 'I told them who you were and what you did. I'm not responsible for any conclusion they might have jumped to. They wish the best for me and obviously like you. To them it's a natural progression.'

She could see that, but it hardly helped. 'You'll have to tell them they're wrong,' she insisted, and watched his eyebrows lift.

'I could, but they'll only be more convinced. You and I give off sparks, Red. They'll never believe we're indifferent to each other.'

'But there has to be a way,' she groaned.

Lucas's smile faded from his eyes. 'There is. We could tell them all we want to do is jump into bed with each other. However, I prefer not to shatter their romantic notions. If you insist, you'll have to do it yourself,' he said frostily, walking past her to go and throw an arm around Peggy and say something which made her laugh.

Megan was left to take her seat, knowing she had deserved his scorn. Knowing, too, that she could not do what he'd suggested. It might be true, but she'd rather nobody else knew just how basic their attraction was. Besides, for one afternoon it wouldn't hurt. She wasn't abandoning her position, just redefining the lines.

It was a wonderful meal, and Megan found herself relaxing although she hadn't thought she would. Lucas acted as if nothing had happened, but she was aware of the coolness in his eyes when he looked her way. Strangely enough, when she should have been welcoming it, she found herself regretting having put it there. She concentrated on the boys, listening to their tales of mischief and mayhem. By the time they began clearing up, the twins had wormed their way into her heart, and there was no getting them out.

Afterwards, the boys insisted on a game of cricket, and for the next hour she found herself caught up in the wildest game she could ever remember playing. She called a halt then, collapsing onto a lounger. Not long afterwards, Peggy joined her, and they watched the game proceed without them.

'It's been nice having you here, Megan. It's good to see Lucas so relaxed,' Peggy remarked after a while. 'He worked so hard to get the company recognised worldwide, he forgot to take time off for himself.'

Megan watched Lucas allow himself to get run out by Martin. 'He's making up for it now with all the women he takes out,' she drawled with an unconscious edge to her voice which Peggy recognised.

'He plays hard, I know, but from the moment he finds the right woman you won't see him with any other. You can take my word for it!' Peggy declared forthrightly, and Megan had to smile.

The other woman was trying to reassure her that she had nothing to worry about, and Megan couldn't utter the words to refute it. Lucas was lucky to have such a loyal champion. 'I believe you, Peggy,' was all she said, and found her hand being squeezed before Peggy glanced at her watch and scrambled to her feet.

'I'll be back in a moment,' she excused herself, hurrying indoors.

Megan sighed and closed her eyes. It was warm, she had been well fed, and knew herself to be amongst friends. For the first time in ages she felt truly at ease. She sank a little lower on the chair, and must have drifted off, because some time later a sharp cry jerked her back to consciousness.

'Uh-oh,' Peggy groaned from beside her. 'Here, hold Annie for me, Megan. I'd better go and see who's hurt.'

Before Megan fully comprehended what was going on, a warm bundle had been placed in her arms and Peggy was trotting off across the grass. The bundle gurgled, and she found herself blinking down into the warm brown eyes of a tiny baby girl. Shock sent her rigid. Everything within her cried out, No! The one thing she had never been able to bring herself to do was hold a baby in her arms. It was a defence mechanism. As long as she'd kept her distance from those tiny scraps of life, she'd known she would be safe from the pain. And now here, suddenly, the very worst had happened.

She wanted to run, but there was no strength in her legs. She was totally disarmed by the tiny, trusting form. Horror made her heart race sickeningly. Then Annie smiled up at her, and deep inside her something cracked wide open. She gasped back a sob, and a tiny hand stretched out towards her face. With a strangled sound Megan found herself lifting her own trembling hand to take the smaller one, feeling her heart clench as those sausage-like fingers instantly clamped about one of hers.

Oh, dear God.

She closed her eyes and lowered her head until her cheek was gently touching the velvety one. Breathing was painful, but with it came the warm baby scents she had tried so hard to block out. It devastated her, and at the same time filled her with such aching tenderness that she felt she might explode with all the emotions going through her. Yet she didn't. Somewhere amongst it all came a deep sense of peace, and she opened her eyes, staring wonderingly at the little girl. Very slowly, she smiled.

She was so beautiful, so perfect. Eyes glittering like emeralds, Megan raised each tiny hand to her lips and kissed it gently, whilst Annie looked at her solemnly, as if she realised this was a momentous occasion for the woman who held her. All Megan's defences fell away like so many dried leaves in autumn as she stroked Annie's downy hair. She knew now that by locking her heart away she had hurt herself far more than anyone else could. She loved babies, and denying it because she wouldn't have any of her own only increased the pain.

A simple act had freed her from that torture, and she accepted the freedom gladly, drowning in a wealth of sensations, until she had to rise up and take a breath, and found herself speared on the end of an electric blue gaze. Lucas was no more than a yard or two away, standing so still, it was as if he had been afraid to move. A shock went through her at the strange expression on his face, and then he smiled and she found herself smiling back.

'Are the boys OK?' she asked, her voice sounding as rusty as if it hadn't been used in years rather than minutes.

'They'll have some bruises tomorrow, but that's par for the course for them,' he reported, coming to sit on the lounger Peggy had abandoned. 'Do you want me to take her?'

Megan glanced down at the little girl who was happily gumming her own fist. 'No, I. . .I think I'd like to hold her for a while, if that's OK?'

Lucas breathed in audibly, raising an eyebrow at Peggy and the family, who had come to join them. 'Sure. Take as long as you like,' he agreed, when the baby's mother nodded.

'When she starts becoming a nuisance you can give her back to me,' Peggy added for good measure, exchanging meaningful looks with her husband. As one they moved away towards the house.

'Mummy, why is Aunty Megan crying?' Michael's piercing treble piped up, and Peggy groaned.

'Oh, Michael! If I didn't love you so much, I would have drowned you at birth!' she exclaimed, dragging her son away to shut him up with ice cream.

For her part, Megan raised a hand to her cheek and felt the moisture there. She hadn't realised that silent tears had slipped from her eyes. No wonder everyone was looking at her so oddly. They must think her a complete idiot, she thought, and cast a glance Lucas's way. But he was lying back on the lounger, his eyes closed as he soaked up the sun. She relaxed again, with a sigh.

Time passed without Megan having a conscious thought. That would come, but right now she was content simply to sit and absorb the glimpse of paradise she had amazingly been allowed. Nobody disturbed her, but she was conscious of Lucas's reassuring presence beside her. She couldn't explain exactly how it made her feel, only that his being there felt so right.

Eventually Peggy came back, and Megan gave up the little girl with a pang of regret. 'She's beautiful, Peggy. I envy you,' she said huskily.

Placing her daughter in a baby chair, Peggy adjusted the shade to keep the sun off her. 'You'll have a baby of your own one day.'

The words cut with a surgeon's precision. With her defences down, Megan couldn't keep the pain from darkening her eyes. She felt emotion choke her, and abruptly jumped to her feet.

'It's awfully quiet. Where is everyone?' she asked jerkily, causing the other woman to frown at her as she straightened.

'Are you all right, Megan?' she asked in concern.

Megan was very much aware that she wasn't all right. Her insides were shaking badly, but she did her best to pull herself together. 'Of course I'm all right. Why shouldn't I be?' she challenged, with a laugh that fell away discordantly. Feeling eyes on her, she turned to find Lucas sitting up and watching her expressionlessly.

'Take it easy, Red,' he said softly.

It was an innocuous enough thing to say, yet it caused something to snap inside her. 'Don't tell me to take it easy!' she shot back at him. 'What the hell do you know about how I feel?'

He stood up slowly, as if aware that any sudden move might make her bolt. 'You're right, I don't know. So why don't you tell me?'

She stared at him, standing there offering to listen, and the rage went out of her as quickly as it had come. He was offering her a shoulder to cry on, and his shoulders were certainly broad enough to bear anything, but she could not do it. She couldn't bear to see the pity fill his beautiful blue eyes. Pity was the one thing she could not accept from anyone. She'd carried her secret this long. She would carry it for ever.

She took a deep breath, feeling herself steadying by the second. 'There's nothing to tell. I think the accident shook me up more than I thought.'

She glanced at Peggy, who smiled and immediately stepped into the breach. 'I know what you need: a good cup of tea. Whenever I've felt a bit wobbly, a cuppa has done me the world of good.'

'I'll give you a hand,' Megan said firmly, walking away from the eyes she could feel burning into her back. When she glanced round a few seconds later, Lucas was talking to the baby. She bit her lip, sadly aware that she had made the mistake of overreacting and that Lucas was piqued enough to wonder why.

'You know if something is worrying you, Lucas really is the person to help,' Peggy remarked softly, drawing Megan's gaze.

Megan sighed tiredly. It had been an emotionally exhausting day, and a dull ache was starting up behind her eyes. 'He can't,' she denied firmly, then smiled at the other woman's troubled expression. 'No one can, Peggy. Believe me, there are just some things in this world that nobody can do anything about. Now, let's make that tea. I really can do with it, and I'd like to play with the twins a little before we go.'

'All right, Megan,' Peggy accepted reluctantly. 'But I want you to know that, even if we can't help, we can be here for you if you ever need us. You're welcome any time.'

The generous offer brought a lump to her throat. 'I might just take you up on it one day,' Megan responded, and that was the last either of them said on the subject.

They stayed for tea and scones, then Lucas declared that they really had to go. In the end, Megan was sorry to leave, for despite everything she had enjoyed the afternoon. The whole family saw them off, and she waved until they turned a bend in the road and the cottage was lost to view. She sank back into her seat then, aware that the nagging headache had increased its tempo. She hoped it wasn't going to develop into a full-blown migraine. She got them occasionally, usually brought on by stress, and the afternoon had been nothing if not stressful in parts.

Lucas concentrated on his driving, and it wasn't until they were almost home that he finally chose to break his self-imposed silence.

'You aren't going to tell me why Aunty Megan was crying, are you?' he asked idly, sending alarm shooting through her system.

She tensed, wondering where this was leading. 'No.' Out of the corner of her eye, she saw his lips twist wryly.

'I thought not. In fact, you aren't going to answer any questions, are you?'

Her own lips curved. 'That would rather depend on the question,' she replied evasively.

'Mmm, so if I was to ask you if you enjoyed yourself you would say. . .?'

'I enjoyed myself very much. They're a nice family,' Megan declared without hesitation.

Lucas shot her a considering look. 'But if I were to ask you why Annie made you look as if the world had come to an end. . .?'

The amusement left her as she realised just how much he had seen. 'I would say you were imagining things.'

'And can we please drop the subject, right?' Lucas added drily. 'OK, let me put it another way. For a woman who professes not to possess a maternal instinct, you held that baby as if she was the most precious thing you had ever seen.'

Megan swallowed to moisten a suddenly dry throat. Lord, just how much had she given away? 'Maternal instinct has nothing to do with it. I was afraid of dropping her.'

They reached the house and he pulled the car into the drive, switching off the engine, leaving them in sudden silence. 'You're lying, Red.'

Though she reached for the door-lock, she knew she had to say something. 'Why would I lie?'

Lucas turned in his seat to stare at her broodingly. 'That's just it—I don't know. But every instinct I have tells me you are. There's something you're not telling me.'

Megan welcomed the spurt of anger that that roused in her. 'You're forgetting something, Lucas. Lying or not, there's no reason for me to tell you anything. You don't own me. I'm not accountable to you.'

'Nevertheless, you will tell me.'

She caught her breath. 'Because you say so? I don't think so!' she shot back, thrusting open the door and climbing out.

Lucas moved just as swiftly, and faced her over the car roof. 'What are you afraid of?'

Megan sighed, dragging her hands through her hair as if that might ease the growing tension beneath her scalp. 'Let it go, Lucas. Sometimes the best thing you can do is walk away. So please, if you think anything of me at all, then just let it be.'

He looked grim suddenly. 'And if I won't?'

'Then damn you!' she said tautly, and turned her back on him, going inside and up to her room. The house was stuffy from being shut up all day and she threw her bedroom windows wide to catch what breeze there was.

She tried lying down, but she was too tense to rest, even though she knew it would be good for her. So much had happened in such a short space of time that she felt as battered as a punching-bag. She wished she had handled everything better, but she could never have anticipated Annie, and the emotional trauma she would produce. However tempted she might be to confide in someone, she knew she wouldn't, for no amount of sympathy could help her.

Restlessly she moved about the room, wondering what Lucas was doing. She wanted to avoid him until she had made the necessary repairs to her stricken defences. He was too astute, and that, she thought, with a wry smile, did frighten her. She didn't know why he couldn't leave her alone, but knew he saw her as a mystery he wanted to solve. It didn't occur to him that the mystery which intrigued him was anguish for her. He would keep on digging away until he had solved it to his satisfaction, leaving her to deal with the mess he left behind.

Only it wasn't going to be that way if she could help it, she decided as she changed into jeans and a shirt. She couldn't rest, so she might as well go down to the yard and do some work. Work had been the ultimate panacea in the early days, the only thing which took her mind off her troubles, and it was no less true now. Catching up her bag, she went downstairs again. She didn't know where Lucas had got to, but she saw no sign of him on her way out to her car and was grateful.

The yard was deserted when she unlocked the gate and walked in. Ted had gone home ages ago. She usually didn't mind the quiet, finding it soothing, like her work. Only this time it proved to be different. She climbed onto her stool and picked up her pencil, following the lines she had drawn with a knowing eye. This was her baby, her brainchild, and it would be flawless. Totally without blemish.

She didn't know she was crying until a teardrop landed on the paper. Others followed, and her breath caught on a racking sob. Unable to stop, she dropped the pencil and buried her head in her hands, crying as if her heart would break, knowing that it already had. Virtually blinded, she stumbled to the nearby couch and collapsed onto it, knowing these tears had been eight long years in coming. She had never cried. She had made her decision, abandoning her dreams, and never once mourned the loss of what had been a vital part of her. This afternoon, holding Annie had torn open the shields she had locked her heart behind, and she cried out all the bottled-up anger and pain.

How long she cried she didn't know, and afterwards she fell into an exhausted sleep. What eventually stirred her was the piercing pain in her head. She recognised it at once for what it was: the migraine she had suspected. The emotional trauma, followed by a long-overdue bout of crying, had brought about the thing she had hoped to avoid. She needed her medication, but it was back at the house. Yet she had to try and get there, for if she didn't the pain would be all the worse.

Groaning, she pushed herself into a sitting position, breathing deeply to combat the rising nausea, closing her eyes as the room spun and shafts of pain lanced into her from the light hitting her eyes.

She knew then that she had left it too late. There was no way she could drive like this. That only left the telephone. She doubted if Daniel would be in, but Lucas had been at the house, and though she would rather not call him she wasn't stupid enough to suffer pain out of sheer pride. With a superhuman effort she somehow got to her feet, but the floor had become like jelly, bouncing under her. She managed two steps before her knees buckled and she crumpled to the floor.

She groaned again, longing for her bed and the dark, and as she lay there gathering her strength to try again she thought she heard her name being called. Freezing, she listened intently, and sure enough there it was again, followed by the sound of footsteps.

'Megan?'

It was Lucas. She didn't know what had brought him here, but right now all she cared about was that help was at hand. 'In here,' she called croakily, and seconds later he was there in the room.

'Megan?' His voice was sharp with concern. 'What happened? Are you hurt?' he demanded, dropping to his knees and bending to turn her gently over.

Megan went rigid, the breath hissing through her teeth as she pressed a hand to her temple. 'Migraine,' she bit out, sighing faintly when Lucas put his palm on her forehead as it felt blessedly cool.

'I thought you'd been attacked,' he growled fiercely, not missing the signs of the tears she had shed. Whether they were the result of the pain or the cause of it he couldn't tell. 'Do you have something you can take?'

'Tablets. Up at the house,' she informed him shortly, and in the next instant she felt herself being lifted then placed back on the couch.

'Right, I'll go and get them.'

'No. Wait!' Megan halted him. 'I'll come with you. I left my car round the back,' she said, getting to her feet by dint of holding onto the arm, and standing swaying even then.

Lucas's eyes narrowed. 'You're not driving like this. You'll wrap yourself round a tree!'

She glared at him through her agony. 'I'm not that

stupid! You can drive—just stop wasting time,' she ordered.

'Gracious to the last!' he drawled mockingly.

She knew she had been rude, but the pain was increasing by leaps and bounds. When she looked at him, her eyes revealed the fact. 'Just get me up to the house, Lucas, please,' she gasped.

He didn't hesitate. 'Stay there; I'll bring the car round,' he ordered, and left her propped against the wall.

Licking her lips, Megan waited until he was gone then made her way unsteadily to her desk, picking up her bag and the office keys. By the time Lucas swung her car to a halt in front of the office, Megan had locked up and was leaning against the doorframe.

'I told you to stay where you were,' he reminded her as he climbed out, swung her up into his arms and carried her to the car. 'Don't you ever obey orders?'

'No,' she retorted, but sank into the seat with a sigh of relief.

'You're more trouble than you're worth. The next time you fall down I might not pick you up,' he warned, but she could hear the concern in his voice and was warmed by it. He joined her and set the car in motion again. 'Which could be any time. You aren't seeing yourself from my point of view!'

'Bad, hmm?' she asked, resting her head on the back of the seat and wincing at the tiniest bump.

'I've seen corpses with more colour!' he said drolly, keeping one eye on the road and the other on her. 'Does this happen often?'

'No.' Thank goodness, she added silently. 'Put it down to all the stress and strain I've been suffering lately.'

'Hmm,' Lucas mused. 'I saw you'd been crying. When you're feeling better, I really think we should talk, Red,' he added gently but firmly.

She didn't have the energy to fight him, and sighed with relief as they drew up before the house, making an answer unnecessary. She didn't protest when he carried her indoors. His arms about her were so strong and protective that strange things were happening inside her. She wished she felt well enough to appreciate it better. Then pain closed in again, and she closed her eyes on a groan as he began to mount the stairs. She wasn't exactly thistledown, yet he wasn't even breathing hard.

'You're very strong,' Megan murmured huskily. 'You make me feel very safe,' she added, not really aware of what she was saying, simply talking to distract herself.

Lucas let out a snort of laughter. 'You sure do pick your moments, Red.'

'I don't know what you mean,' she muttered, aware that he held her fractionally closer.

'I mean you're the most luscious bundle I've carried upstairs for a long time, and I'm taking you to your bedroom. It isn't the time for you to start flirting with me.'

She thought he sounded amused. 'Is that what I was doing?'

'Tell me again when you're feeling better and we'll take it from there,' Lucas advised, nudging open her bedroom door. Walking to the bed, he laid her down gently on the covers. 'Where are the pills, Megan?'

She winced as she lifted her head and pointed to the drawer of her bedside table. Seconds later Lucas held the bottle. Reading the label, he shook out the correct dosage and went to get a glass of water from the bathroom. With an arm steadying her shoulders, he helped her swallow the medication before easing her back onto the pillow.

Megan watched him cross to the windows and pull the curtains, sighing with relief as the light was dimmed and the pain in her eyes eased fractionally. It occurred to her then that he had turned up in the nick of time, yet he couldn't have known she was in trouble. 'Why did you come to the yard?'

'I was looking for you. I thought you might be upset, and I wanted to apologise. When I couldn't find you in the house, I tried the yard.'

She sighed heavily. 'You don't have to worry about me, Lucas. I can take care of myself.'

'I noticed,' he countered drily, coming back to the bed. 'I can't help worrying about you, Red. I think it's about time somebody did. Now, let's get these clothes off you. You'll feel better in bed.'

Megan knew she would, but the idea of Lucas removing her clothes sent the blood pounding through her head in alarm. She struggled to sit up. 'I can do it,' she argued, but Lucas pushed her back down.

'It will be quicker if I do it. Stop arguing for once, Red, and allow someone to help you,' he ordered shortly, and made quick work of removing her outer clothes. Then, when she was clad only in the skimpiest of underwear, he shifted her so that he could pull the duvet out from under her and replace it over her trembling body.

'Better?' he asked softly.

Megan was glad of the gloom, for it hid the heat in her cheeks. He had been totally impersonal, so there should have been no reason for her to be trembling, yet she was, and the pain in her head had nothing to do with it. 'Yes. Thank you.' The words were slightly slurred as the powerful painkillers began to take effect.

'Go to sleep, Megan. I'll look in on you later,' he promised, and as he headed for the door her eyes were already closing.

Lucas didn't leave, only made sure the door was shut before pulling her chair up beside the bed and sitting down. His eyes remained broodingly on her face, seeing the pain she was suffering, and beyond it a sadness that she probably wasn't even aware of.

He knew he had made the mistake of taking her at face value, seeing only the pest of a kid he had grown up with. Yet he realised now that she was a mass of contradictions. On the one hand she was cold, on the other incredibly passionate. Outwardly she gave the impression of being a woman in control of her life, and yet today she had looked so vulnerable that his heart had very nearly stopped. Nothing about Megan Terrell was as it should be, and he wanted to get to the bottom of it. No, *needed* to get to the bottom of it. He hadn't realised how desperately he wanted her to trust him, to confide in him, until she'd absolutely refused to.

Sighing, he stretched out his long legs, prepared to stay and watch over her. As he had told her, somebody had to, because beneath that iron veneer she was a vulnerable woman, and he wanted to protect her. He was surprised by just how much he wanted that, but he knew himself well enough to go with it. Something told him that the rewards would be worth the trouble.

CHAPTER SEVEN

MEGAN stirred, slowly drifting towards wakefulness, and as she did so two things registered in her fuzzy brain. Her pillow had grown hard and her head was still thumping. Usually the tablets knocked her out, so that when she woke the pain had gone, leaving her feeling hungover but recovering. This was different, and, frowning, she opened her eyes carefully, prepared to shut them quickly if the light hurt. Instead, what she saw had them widening. The reason her pillow was hard was because it had metamorphosed into Lucas's chest. The thumping she could hear was not her headache but the regular beat of his heart.

Shock rocketed through her. She couldn't imagine how Lucas—a virtually naked Lucas, her equally naked limbs were telling her—had come to be in her bed. Neither did she know how she had come to curl herself up against him so trustingly. Yet she had, and as her senses began to operate she peeped beneath the covers, and was relieved to find that they were both wearing underwear, even if it did nothing to disguise the shape and feel of the body underneath. Awareness set her nerve-ends tingling like crazy, sending messages to her brain which started a sensual glow inside her.

She knew she ought to move, for the position was extremely compromising, but the warmth and scent of him urged her to linger and savour a moment which would not come again. The temptation to run her hand over the smooth, taut flesh of his belly was strong, and she was fighting a losing battle when, from above her head, she heard Lucas sigh. Instantly she attempted to wriggle away to the safety of the edge of the bed, but a strong arm snaked up around her waist to prevent her.

Megan lost her breath, and barely had time to look up into glittering blue eyes before she was held against him, his lips brushing the warm flesh of her shoulder to devastating effect. She had to bite down hard on her lip to withhold a tiny moan.

'Mmm, you taste nice,' Lucas murmured drowsily, his free hand coming to rest on the curve of her hip. 'You're warm and soft, too. I think I like waking up like this,' he groaned, and her pulse rate shot off the scale.

It was stomach-twisting to realise that she liked it too. The outside world seemed a million miles away, this closeness the only reality. In the darkness before dawn, nothing else seemed to matter.

'How's the head?' he enquired softly, brushing his lips against her temple, and even as she shivered faintly in response his words brought her down to earth.

'It's fine,' Megan replied in a voice which was supposed to be cool, but sounded anything but. 'Lucas, I don't know how we came to be here like this, but you have to go,' she ordered shakily, pushing away enough to be able to see his face.

He was smiling faintly. 'We're here like this, Red, precisely because last night you refused to let me go,' he informed her shockingly.

Her lips parted in a gasp. 'I couldn't have!' she protested, even as the tiniest sliver of a memory fluttered in and out of her mind.

Lucas raised his hand and stroked her hair from her face. 'You don't remember asking me to stay? You told me you didn't want to be alone any more.'

Those last two words speared her heart, they were so revealing. Dear Lord, what else had she said and done? 'I—' Her throat closed over.

He hushed her with a finger on her lips. 'It's OK.

You wanted comfort, Red, and I was happy to give it. Where's the harm in that?'

Her lashes dropped. The harm was in knowing it was pointless to want things like this. To take comfort now would only make the loss sharper later on. And yet something inside her cried out for human warmth.

'It's wrong,' she muttered gruffly, trying to convince herself more than him.

Lucas only held her closer, his hand gliding gently down her spine. 'How can it be wrong?' he growled throatily. 'It sure as hell feels right to me. I want you here, and this is where you want to be too, don't you?'

She did, God help her, because it felt more than right. Yet it went against every rule she had made. Rules designed to save her sanity in a world gone suddenly mad. What price anything if she broke them now?

'You have to go!' she insisted breathlessly, feeling the heat coming from him turning her bones to water.

Lucas raised his head at that, and she found herself staring heart-stoppingly into fathomless blue eyes. 'And if I won't?' he countered, his voice a gravelly whisper which teased its way along her nerves.

Prickly heat broke out all over her flesh. 'Lucas, please!' she protested, only to watch as a beautifully lazy smile spread across his lips before he bent down to nuzzle the velvety skin of her neck. She forgot to breathe.

'I long to please you, darling. Just tell me what you want me to do,' he declared seductively, and she took a gasping breath as her senses came perilously close to rioting. She had to get away, or. . .

Instinctively her hands rose to push him away, but only came into contact with warm male flesh. Her breath caught in her throat as a dozen messages were transmitted to her brain, none of them sane, and she closed her eyes in desperation. But that only served to magnify the sensations which his exploring lips were producing. He was tracing a path up to her ear, sending shivers down her spine, turning up a heat that made her insides begin to melt. And she wanted to melt so badly that she knew that if she didn't stop him her already shaky defences would crumble into dust.

With an almost audible groan she made herself fight on. 'S-stop it, Lucas.'

He raised his head, but didn't release her. The sensual curve of his lips so tantalisingly close to hers was a refinement of torture. 'We have to finish this, Red, you know that.'

Her heart lurched and her eyes locked with his. 'It should never have begun,' she groaned, curling her hands into fists to prevent them from spreading across the strong planes of his shoulders.

Lucas shook his head, dipping it to kiss the corner of her lips before lifting it again to study the result of his foray with a brooding intensity. 'Maybe, but it's gone too far for us to go back. We want each other, Red. When I look at you my heart pounds and my stomach twists into knots. I ache for the warmth of you, and I know you feel the same.' He paused to trace one finger over the trembling fullness of her bottom lip. 'Why deny ourselves what we both need?'

Megan's heart pounded. Would it be so wrong? He was right, she wanted him, so why deny herself when she didn't have to? A brief affair with Lucas wouldn't hurt him because he did not want a commitment with her. It would not be like before. No way would it be the same because she wanted Lucas with a passion she hadn't known she possessed. There was nothing to hold her back except her scruples, and they had suddenly become redundant. For once in her life, she could let her defences drop without fear of the consequences. It was more than she'd ever expected, and she knew she would always regret it if she didn't reach out and grasp this moment with both hands.

Her head swam with the sense of freedom. Every breath she took dragged in the scent of him, heightening her senses. Her gaze dropped to his tanned torso, and she trembled like a leaf in the wind as need rippled through her. She wanted to press her lips to his heated flesh and taste him, know him, to assuage a burning craving to absorb him into her.

'Do it,' Lucas urged softly, and her nerves jolted violently.

'What?' she croaked back. Was he a mind-reader too?

'Touch me. Do anything you like,' he invited. When she hesitated, he raised her chin with his thumb. 'I want you to touch me, Red,' he insisted in a thickened tone. 'Don't you know I've been aching for you to?' he breathed, and lowered his head again.

It was like drowning, and Megan was going down for the third time. His kiss was a piercingly sweet persuasion against which she quickly discovered she had no defence. His lips enticed her to join him, to share in sensations so exquisite that she couldn't withhold the whimper of pleasure which escaped her tight throat.

With a soft sigh, her arms slipped about his neck, where they had always wanted to be, and she opened to him, welcoming the deep invasion of his tongue. She expected instant passion—the flash fire which overcame them every time they touched—but Lucas had other ideas. He was holding back, using every ounce of his considerable control as he tasted her, pleasured the deepest, most sensitive recesses, and invited her tongue to mate with his in sensually silken strokes.

Megan was lost in an instant. Her one brief affair had never offered her this enchantment of the senses. She had always suspected that Lucas was a magnificent lover, but nothing could have prepared her for the reality. She gave herself up to his undoubted mastery.

Lucas abandoned her lips to trace delicate kisses over her cheeks and eyes, then on down to the arched column of her neck. Behind her closed lids, Megan was dazed by a kaleidoscopic explosion of colours. His hand was so gentle as it discovered the fragile bones of her shoulder that she scarcely felt it, and yet not one part of her remained untouched by it. She held her breath as he lifted his head and watched his fingers tracing the tender skin of her arm until he reached her hand and raised it, bringing each finger separately to his lips before pressing a final one to her palm.

'So beautiful,' he murmured softly, and lowered his lips to the scented valley between her breasts.

A groan escaped her and she felt herself burning up. Sweet heaven, but he seemed intent on driving her out of her mind! She could not lie still. Her hands rose to his hair, gliding into the silky mass and rejoicing at the way it curled around her fingers. He found the catch of her bra, and she gasped, her body turning fluid as he stripped it from her.

Her breathing turned ragged, but Lucas's control was awesome as he traversed the planes of her belly and thighs with his hands and mouth. Her hips moved instinctively as he brushed away her final covering, and she began to tremble at the sheer beauty of what he was doing to her. He kissed the backs of her knees, her instep, and she hadn't known they could be so sensitive, as he glided down one silken leg and up the other. He moved with exquisite slowness, learning her, tasting her, making her heart pound and an ache begin to throb deep inside her.

'Every inch of you is perfect,' Lucas declared as he eased away from her to remove his shorts. His hands spanned her waist, and very slowly rose towards her breasts, which were swollen and aching for his touch.

She bit her lip when he paused short of his goal, lifting his eyes to hers.

'Last chance, Red. If this isn't what you want, say so and I'll stop. But, God help me, beyond this point I don't think I'll be able to.'

Any more than she could. 'If you stop now, I think I'll kill you, Lucas Canfield!' she groaned, and it was all the encouragement he needed.

The passion he had held back was released in all its magnificent glory and, catching her tightly to him, he kissed her with aching need. The pleasure she had felt only minutes earlier was nothing to this. Before he had touched her as if he had found a lost treasure; now she was all woman, and he needed her.

A cry of pleasure escaped her as this time he set about showing her exactly how much he wanted her. Released from the spell she had been under, Megan was free to do the same. They couldn't get enough of each other. Hands and lips were everywhere as they gasped and moaned by turns, and it was a visceral pleasure to hear Lucas groan and feel him tremble when she touched him.

She gasped when he found her breast, feeling her aching flesh swell into the cup of his hand, her nipple hardening into a point which thrust into his palm. His thumb moved, rubbing back and forth until she couldn't withhold a moan of pleasure as coils of tension twisted deep inside her. Then his mouth replaced his hand, his tongue laving the sensitised nub until finally he drew it into the moist cavern of his mouth and suckled strongly.

As her other breast suffered the same mind-blowing torture, her own hands were exploring, tracing down his spine until she found his buttocks and pulled him against her, her hips moving in an age-old invitation. Then her hands slipped between them, finding the hardness of him, running her fingers along the velvety length until Lucas groaned and his own hand dragged her away. All then became a glorious storm of sighs and groans as damp flesh rubbed against damp flesh. Limbs entwined until it was hard to know where one ended and the other began.

When they could take no more, Lucas moved over her, parting her thighs, entering her with a shuddering sigh which measured the scantness of his control. Megan had lost hers long ago, and her legs rose, clasping about his hips, urging him deeper, meeting his thrusts with tiny cries which rose to a crescendo as the tempo increased in the final surge.

As, with a cry, Megan was forced out over the edge, the world exploded around her. She was dizzily aware of Lucas stiffening as he too climaxed and joined her with a guttural cry, his arms holding her crushed to him. Megan clung on, feeling weightless, boneless, aware of nothing but the pleasure to be found in this one pair of arms.

When they finally returned to the heated darkness of the bed, neither had the strength to move away. She didn't mind. She loved the feel of him, and his weight was nothing. Yet from somewhere Lucas found the strength to move onto his side, easing her with him so that they still touched from head to toe.

Her hand went to his cheek, her head into the curve of his shoulder. Replete, she slept.

The next time Megan woke, it was light. Lucas still slept, and she lay watching him, filled with a serenity she hadn't known before. He looked younger in sleep, more rested and carefree. She was tempted to reach out and brush away a stray wisp of hair which had tumbled onto his forehead, but didn't want to disturb him.

Her heart swelled with emotion. She wanted to preserve this moment for ever, because it felt so right, so perfect. She had no regrets. Making love with Lucas had been the most magical experience of her life. She sighed contentedly. The steady beat of Lucas's heart was reassuring, his arm curving her waist protective. A sense of peace stole over her, so profound that she realised that what she had previously taken for that emotion had been a mere shadow of reality. She experienced it now because she was, quite simply, where she had always wanted to be.

Always? The concept rocked her with all the force of a powerful explosion. Disarmed by the contentment which filled her, she found the truth breaking through the remnants of her defences and shining like purest crystal. Yes, always—for she loved him. Boundlessly. Wholeheartedly.

It was perfectly clear now why she had continually ragged Lucas about his love life. The cause had been pure, instinctive jealousy. Instinctive because although she hadn't known it she had loved him even then. Now she had the explanation of why she had felt so alive these past few days. She had fallen in love with him on sight. The sense of peace she felt now came from realising she had finally come home.

There was no place she would rather be, nobody she would rather be with. Lucas was her destiny, and she wanted to stay with him for ever. But, even as a smile curved her lips, a drop of ice was forming in her heart, rending the fabric of that peace irreparably. Reality raised its ugly head, and would not be denied.

There was no home for her with anyone, and especially not with Lucas. To him this was just a romantic interlude. Last night, in her ignorance, she had thought it was the same for her. A once-in-a-lifetime opportunity to have some memories to cherish without any risk. Now she knew differently. Her emotions were involved, and that changed everything. Cruel fingers clutched at her heart, starting up an ache which no painkiller could deaden. How blind she had been. Lucas was everything she had ever wanted.

She felt the happiness trickle out of her, draining the rainbow hues from her radiant heart until all that remained was a despairing grey. He was everything she could never have. Not for ever, and not in the short term either.

There was no way she could have an affair with him now. To go on would only be to store up pain for herself, and she had already suffered enough pain for two lifetimes. Only by breaking off now could she limit the damage, for leaving it until the end would surely devastate her. Even now she hurt so much that she wanted to cry out, and it could only grow to an intensity which would shatter her. In a lifetime of painful decisions that had diminished her bit by bit, she now had to make the one which left the future bleak and empty.

Last night had to be the beginning and the end. She closed her eyes, wishing she could put the clock back, to save herself from the awful knowledge that, for her peace of mind, last night had been far, far too much. Whilst for her heart it would never, ever be enough.

Who would have thought it would come to this? An affair with Lucas had seemed to offer a moment out of time. Something to be looked back on with fondness and no regrets. It had blown up in her face all too soon, and now she had to extricate herself from this mess she had made. She knew she was going to have to put on the act of her life. Lucas must never know she loved him. They had shared a mutual desire which last night had satisfied. That was all. Hardly a novel situation for him. He'd probably shrug it off. It certainly wouldn't break his heart.

Hers, on the other hand, was in bad shape, and if she wanted to protect it then she must not be lying there when he woke up. Finding it one of the hardest things she had ever had to do, Megan carefully slipped from beneath his arm and slid from the bed. She turned her back on him mentally and physically, gathering up fresh clothes and shoes and hastening into the bathroom. She was determined not to cry, because that served no purpose. She knew what she had to do, so she must grit her teeth and get on with it.

She showered quickly, afraid that the noise might stir him, and once dressed she let herself back into the bedroom. Lucas hadn't moved, and with her heart in her eyes she allowed herself one last look.

She stepped closer to the sleeping form. Something inside her felt ready to burst. She had to say it, just once. Her voice was the merest breath of a whisper. 'I love you, Lucas. God help me, but I do. I. . .' Her throat closed over, and she pressed trembling lips together, turning away and slipping out into the corridor before she was tempted to do something really silly, like fling herself at him.

Wretchedly near to the forbidden tears, she hurried downstairs. The thought of breakfast turned her stomach over, so she avoided the kitchen and went in search of her car. She would go to the office, even though it was Saturday. Work had always helped in the past, and it was all she had to distract her on a quiet, sunny morning. The sun was an affront. After what she had just discovered, it should have been raining. Some days things never worked out right.

A little while later, she parked next to Lucas's car where he had abandoned it in order to help her the day before. Had it only been yesterday? It felt like for ever already. She rested her forehead tiredly on the wheel. She'd tried to avoid love, fearing finding herself wanting what she knew she could not have. But love had been cleverer, creeping up on her when she wasn't looking, so that she'd found herself in the middle of it, with no way to avoid the inevitable heartache. The funny thing was, Lucas had nothing to do with it. He'd never asked her to love him. She'd brought it all on herself.

Which, while true, was no comfort at all, she decided wanly as she let herself into the yard. She went to the boat shed first, to see how Ted had been getting on. He really was a wonderful craftsman, bringing her designs to life. Yet today she found no satisfaction in the sight of the half-built craft. Her heart wasn't in it. Her heart was back at the house with a dark-haired, blue-eyed man.

She turned away with a grimace. This was getting too maudlin. She hated self-pity. It was destructive and pointless. Sighing heavily, she left the shed, and was on her way to the office to make herself a cup of coffee when the sound of a car engine made her falter. Her heart thumped as she glanced towards the entrance. Could it be Lucas already? Half of her longed to see him, whilst the other half said it was too soon; she wasn't prepared. As it turned out, it wasn't Lucas who walked through the gate moments later but a total stranger.

He appeared to be in his mid-thirties, was built like a tank, and had a nose which had been broken more than once. Megan felt a shiver of apprehension run down her spine. This was not their usual kind of customer, and somehow she didn't think he wanted to buy a boat. She watched him approach, hiding her nervousness under a polite smile.

'Good morning. Can I help you?' she asked, wishing she weren't the only one there.

The man had a good look round before answering. 'I'm looking for Danny. Is he about?'

Megan caught her breath, alarmingly aware that only Daniel's new friends called him that, but that this man did not look very friendly right now. She didn't know what was going on, but instinctively she knew she had

AMANDA BROWNING141

to play it cool. 'You mean my brother, Daniel? No, he's not here. I've no idea where he is. I haven't seen him since the day before yesterday.'

He took another look round. 'There's another car outside,' he remarked suspiciously, and Megan's heart skipped. She resisted the urge to ask him what business it was of his—he might just tell her.

'That belongs to one of my employees. Daniel's taste runs to something red and flashy. If I see him today, can I give him a message?' she offered coolly, standing her ground. The man finally nodded.

'Yeah, darlin', you can. Tell him Vince wants to see him, sharpish,' he said with a mocking laugh, and, as she caught her breath, turned on his heel and left.

Megan stared after him, feeling distinctly uneasy. When she had sought distraction, this hadn't been what she'd had in mind. That man was bad news, and as she continued on her way to the office her heart thumped. She wondered what Daniel had done now.

The coffee didn't settle her and working was a joke, when her mind was seething like a bubbling pot. She needed to know what was going on and was on the point of going to find her brother when Daniel strolled in. She fully expected him to fling himself into a free chair in his usual manner, but today he crossed to the window and stood staring fixedly out of it, the tension in him so plain, it was almost tangible. What brought a worried frown to her forehead, however, was the fact that he still wore his evening suit from the night before.

'You're up early,' he remarked casually—far too casually for her peace of mind. He was hiding something.

'And you're up late,' she returned evenly. 'I hardly seem to see you these days, Daniel. Where have you been hiding yourself?' She had chosen the words carefully, and it did nothing for her unease to see his back tense even more.

'Don't be ridiculous—I'm not hiding. What have I got to hide from?' he countered edgily, still with his back to her. 'Besides, I've stayed out all night before,' he added, stuffing his hands into his trouser pockets and attempting to look relaxed.

'I know,' she placated him gently. 'It's merely that I just had the strangest encounter.'

'Oh, yes? Of the third kind, was it?'

He might be joking, but he was bracing himself too, and her nerves jangled. What did he think she was going to say? What had he done? 'You had a visitor. He left when you weren't here,' she said levelly, and felt her tension increase with his patent relief.

He cleared his throat quickly, turning towards her, his face a colourless mask. 'Oh, well, I dare say he'll catch up with me later.'

Megan stared at him with a sinking heart. 'That was the impression I got too. He left a message.'

At the mention of that, Daniel looked sick. 'He did?'

'He said Vince wanted to see you. I got the feeling it had better be sooner rather than later. Daniel, what's going on?'

He jumped as if she had jabbed him with a pin. 'Nothing. What gave you that idea?' he denied instantly, and she sent him an old-fashioned look.

'You've been acting like a cat on a hot coal, hardly knowing whether it's better to jump off or stay put!'

He laughed, but it was not a happy sound. 'It's just that I've a lot on my mind,' he said, and came over to her, pulling up a chair and sitting down to lean forward eagerly. 'I've had this amazing idea,' he explained. 'I've been feeling in need of a holiday, and I can't remember the last time you went away, Meg. We could go together. What do you say?' His hand came out to cover hers as it lay on the desk, squeezing it encouragingly.

Megan didn't know what to say. All she could think

was that things must be pretty bad if he was having to resort to this. 'Why now, Daniel?'

His smile was cajoling. 'Because everything's so dead here. I need some fun. We could travel around. Just think of it!'

She was, and it left her cold. She shook her head. 'No.'

He hadn't expected a refusal. 'What do you mean, no?'

Megan gently pulled her hand away. 'I mean no, I won't go on holiday with you.'

Daniel shot to his feet, kicking the chair aside angrily. 'Damn it, I was banking on you. I have to get away!'

She had guessed that much, and it was making her feel very nervous. 'Why?'

For a moment it looked as if he wasn't going to answer, then he dragged a hand through his hair. 'I owe some people some money,' he admitted flatly, and the way he said it made a chill run up her spine.

'What people?'

'Not anyone you'd know. I. . .borrowed some money to place a bet. All I needed was one win and I'd have been able to pay back all my debts!' he exclaimed, as if the fault hadn't been his in gambling in the first place.

Megan tried not to look as alarmed as she felt. 'I take it you lost?'

Daniel laughed raggedly. 'I asked for more time to pay, and they gave me forty-eight hours.'

It was like something out of the worst kind of B movie. 'How much do you owe?'

The amount he quoted made her feel sick. 'The bank won't help, nor any of the other sources I've tried. I've been going out of my mind trying to find a way out, and all my friends have turned their backs on me!'

It was not the time to say, I told you so, although she was tempted. 'Can't you go back to these people and explain the situation?'

'Damn it, Meg, if I go back to them without the money, they'll break my legs, or worse! I have to find some cash, and quick!'

His urgency transmitted itself to her, and she knew instinctively not to doubt it because Daniel was really scared. 'What can you do?'

'Leave the country.'

'If these people are as nasty as you say they are, they'll have long memories. If you went you could never come back,' she said, trying to think clearly but finding it hard as she'd never been in this sort of situation. 'Can't you go to the police? Say you've been threatened?'

Daniel snorted. 'Get real. There was no threat as such; besides, imagine how well that would go down with them. I'd end up as part of the next motorway!'

That wasn't even remotely funny. 'Oh, Daniel, how could you get mixed up with these people?'

'Because I needed the money! Haven't you been listening?'

His anger came from fear, and she pressed her trembling hands together in an effort to hide her own alarm. 'I am listening. I know you need help, but I can't see how I can give it to you.'

He looked up at her then, eyes hopeful. 'That's just it—you can. OK, maybe the holiday wasn't a good idea, but couldn't you use some of your inheritance to help me? I promise to pay it back.'

She bit her lip, knowing she was going to dash his hopes, but she couldn't offer what didn't exist. 'I don't have that sort of money, Daniel,' she said softly, and he frowned irritably.

'Of course you do. You inherited thousands when Dad died.'

'I know,' she agreed grimly. 'But I don't have it any more. How on earth do you imagine this place has kept running? I've been paying the bills with my own money for months now. I'm almost broke, Daniel.'

To give him his due, he looked stricken, and for once it wasn't because of his own problems. 'Good God, why didn't you tell me?' he croaked.

She sighed tiredly. 'Because you haven't been listening.'

Daniel let out a very shaky breath and combed trembling fingers through his dishevelled hair. 'Lord, I'm sorry, Meg,' he apologised, and held her eyes, his own anxious. 'All of it?'

She raised a shoulder resignedly. 'Almost.'

'God!' Daniel groaned, rubbing his hands over his sickly face. When he looked at her again, his eyes were dull. 'It started out as a joke, you know. A bit of a lark. A bet here and there. Then I went to the casino and... the next thing I knew I was hooked. Only instead of winning, I lost. I kept on losing. That's why I went to Vince. He doesn't take kindly to welshers, but I can't pay him back. It's all gone. What am I going to do?'

Megan left her chair and went to him, putting an arm about his shoulders. She could only see one solution. 'I think you should go and talk to Lucas,' she proposed, knowing that Lucas would not refuse to help his friend, but Daniel looked appalled.

'You're joking! How could I tell him what a fool I've been?'

Now he'd admitted what she had known all along! 'You'll have to decide what's more important to you, Daniel. Your pride or your life,' she declared bluntly, and saw his colour come and go.

'You don't pull your punches, do you?'

'Kindness isn't going to help you, but Lucas can. He's your friend. Talk to him, and be honest for once,' Megan urged him.

Daniel sighed, but at least when he looked at her he had more colour. 'You're right. God, I've been an idiot, but I'll make it up to you, I promise. You know, if Lucas lends me the money, this place will have to go.'

She stared at him in dismay. 'But you can't sell Terrell's!' It was her life. What would she do without it? She would have nothing left.

Unaware of her thoughts, Daniel stood up, squaring his shoulders. 'I don't want to, but it may be the only way to pay him back, and you. I know Terrell's means a lot to you, Meg, but you're good enough to work anywhere.'

Megan swallowed hard. She wanted to protest further, but for once Daniel looked more like his old self, and she could not destroy that. 'You must do what you have to, Daniel,' she said huskily, and he gave her a half-smile.

'I'd better go and clean myself up before I see him,' Daniel decided, taking a quick inspection of his crumpled appearance.

'You do look the worse for wear,' she agreed. 'Good luck,' she added softly, and, with a wry look, Daniel took himself off.

Megan crossed to the window, flinging it wide and breathing in a lungful of the warm fresh air. She couldn't lose this place. The one part of her world she had always relied on not to let her down, no matter what else she had had to give up, had been Terrell's. It was her rock. She had given it all the passionate devotion she would have given to her own family, had things turned out differently. It had become a kind of surrogate family, and if she was asked to give that up her life would become barren once more.

Yet it was out of her hands. The whole fabric of her world was slowly crumbling around her, and all she could do was put on a brave face and pretend she didn't care. It ought to have been easy, with all the practice she had had, but it wasn't. Something told her it would never be easy again.

CHAPTER EIGHT

'I THOUGHT I'd find you here.'

Megan jumped at the sound of Lucas's voice. She was sitting on the grass in the tiny bay, lost in her own thoughts. She had locked up the yard hours ago, but hadn't wanted to go home, so she had come here for peace and quiet, and now Lucas had found her.

At once the air became electric, and all her senses sharpened, so that she could almost feel him. Intimate memories flashed into her mind, and she knew she would never be unaware of him again. She wondered how she would live with that, and yet keep it hidden. He was part of her; to deny it made her only half-alive. Yet deny it she must. She had to be strong—for her own good.

'Nice work, Sherlock,' she quipped, glancing round with a mocking smile, only to have her stomach plunge and her heart lurch wildly. Lucas was dressed in the most disreputable thigh-hugging jeans she had ever seen, whilst his shirt was unbuttoned, as if he had just slipped it on, leaving his tanned, muscular torso temptingly bare. Suddenly dry-mouthed, and with her hands prickling with the urge to touch his warm male flesh, she hurriedly turned her gaze back to the river, very much aware that he was crossing the ground towards her.

Sure enough, seconds later he dropped down beside her, stretching out his long legs, taking his weight on his arms. She could feel his eyes on her, but refused to look round, making a pretence of finding the river fascinating, when in fact she saw nothing at all.

'I missed you when I woke up,' he said huskily,

trailing a finger down the velvety flesh of her arm.
'Why didn't you stay?'

His touch made her want to close her eyes, but she
fought it. 'Sorry, but I never could lie in bed when the
sun was up,' she replied coolly, hoping he couldn't hear
the way her heart was hammering.

'I could have made it worth your while,' Lucas
countered seductively, his fingers lingering on the pulse
at her wrist, and she very nearly groaned aloud.

This was worse than she had expected. He was too
good at this, and she was far, far too susceptible. She
had to make him stop, and said the first thing which
came into her head. 'Have you seen Daniel?' she asked,
and felt the stillness in him an instant before his hand
dropped away. Ridiculously she felt bereft, chilled by
the withdrawal she had sought.

'No, I haven't. Should I have?' he replied in a voice
which told her he had registered her mood. By now his
mind would be doing rapid calculations.

She managed an offhand shrug, licking her dry lips
nervously. His eyes were boring into her skull, making
her heart race, and she shifted uncomfortably. 'I sent
him to you.'

'For any particular purpose?' He sounded lazy, but
the vibrations coming off him were anything but. She
knew she couldn't avoid looking at him for ever, and
steeled herself to glance round.

Her eyes were met and held by stormy blue ones.
'Toto ask for your help,' she enlarged faintly. He was
so close, it would take only the smallest effort to reach
out and touch him, to feel his warmth. Yet she couldn't
give herself even that comfort.

'What's going on, Red?' he demanded softly.

'Daniel must tell you himself,' she insisted, just as
Lucas reached out to brush a wisp of hair from
her cheek. She froze instantly, her breath locked in her
throat.

'I'm not talking about Daniel's gambling problem,' he corrected her, and she gasped.

'You know?'

He sent her an old-fashioned look. 'Of course I know. I'm neither blind nor stupid. I've always been able to tell when Dan is in trouble. A telephone call told me what other facilities the club offered, and some careful questioning did the rest. I was hoping he would come to me of his own accord. Which it appears he will, thanks to you. But that isn't what's important right now. You know what is. I want to know what's going on with us, Red.'

The confrontation she had anticipated was upon her with a vengeance, and her lashes dropped, shielding her emotions from his all too perceptive gaze. 'Nothing is going on,' she denied brittlely.

His expression grew sceptical. 'Then why did you run away?'

Because I couldn't stay, her heart answered achingly. Aloud, she set her chin determinedly. 'I didn't run away,' she said, with only the faintest quaver in her voice. 'I told you. I simply got up.'

'Even though we had made love together last night?' His voice had dropped to a lower key which worked on her senses, stirring them up, reminding her of the achingly beautiful loving they had shared.

And, because she was not proof against it, she knew her answer to that had to be totally convincing. To back it up she forced her eyes to meet his in mild consternation. 'What has that to do with anything? We made love. We enjoyed it. End of story.' If only that were true, but she knew this story would run and run. She would not be free of it until the day she died.

Unseen by her, something dangerous flashed in Lucas's eyes for a moment, then was gone, as his face lost all expression. 'I see. So that's it, is it?'

Relieved not to be in the middle of an ugly scene,

Megan enlarged on the tack she had chosen to take. 'You were expecting more?'

His blue eyes narrowed but never left hers. 'Frankly, Red, I was expecting a whole lot more. I enjoyed last night, but it was nowhere near enough.'

Her lashes fluttered. She knew the feeling, but they were experiencing it for different reasons. Hers was love, whilst his was merely desire. Whilst it was flattering to know that Lucas's interest hadn't been satisfied so quickly, it only confirmed how he saw their relationship. She was doing the right thing.

'I'm sorry—' she began, a faint huskiness tingeing her voice, but Lucas interrupted her.

'Sorry doesn't cut it, Red. I'm not some callow youth. I know when a woman wants me, and, sweetheart, you *do* still want me,' he pronounced confidently, making her nerves leap anxiously.

Colour rose in her cheeks and she swallowed hard. Suddenly this was not going the way she had expected. She had decided he would give in gracefully when he realised she wanted to end their brief affair, but for reasons she couldn't fathom he was determined to change her mind. She wouldn't, and even though he was right about her still wanting him she had to convince him he was wrong.

'I think I know better than you what I want, Lucas!' she countered with all the firmness she could muster.

'Why are you denying it? We both know I could make love to you right here and you wouldn't fight me.'

Her senses rioted at the idea and she knew it was true. When he touched her, she melted. She knew she always would. Yet she had to deny it. 'Don't flatter yourself!'

'Do you want me to prove it?' Lucas challenged softly, and her eyes registered her despairing anger.

'It would be against my will!' she choked out, and immediately saw his expression soften.

'I know, Red, and the person you would be fighting is yourself. The question is, why? The air buzzes when we're together. We send sparks off each other even now. We both know it isn't over, so why are you doing this?'

Megan's throat closed over. His understanding of her was uncanny and frightening. It made her feel as if there was nothing he didn't know about her. Yet there was no way he could know that she loved him, and that was the way it had to stay. The affair was over. He *had* to accept it.

'A woman has the right to say no,' she reminded him thickly, and he nodded his acceptance of the fact.

'And the man who cares about her has the right to know why,' he returned, sending alarm signals skittering along her nerves.

Megan caught her breath. What was he saying? She began to feel panic claw at her stomach. No. It wasn't true. They were just words! He couldn't care. He *mustn't* care! Alarm slowly trickled icily into her veins. She had to put an end to this right now. 'You don't care about me, Lucas,' she denied sickly, her heart starting up a faster tempo.

This time there was the faintest hint of a smile in his eyes. 'Don't I, Red? I think I know how I feel better than you do, darling,' he drawled, using her own words against her.

Her colour faded at his insinuation, her alarm increasing in leaps and bounds. 'Don't call me that!'

One eyebrow quirked. 'Why not? It's how I think of you,' he countered at once, and her heart stopped. This couldn't be happening! It was her worst nightmare come to life!

She jumped to her feet, hands bunched into fists at her sides. 'Stop playing games with me!' Tell me that's all it is, she begged silently. Tell me it's just a wicked game!

Lucas was on his feet too, and he wasn't laughing. 'This is no game to me. This is for real. What are you running from, Red? Why can't you trust me enough to tell me?'

She lost her breath. She was going crazy. She had to be, for why else would he have almost sounded as if her lack of trust hurt him? It couldn't be true. She wouldn't let it be true. Lucas didn't care. He was just frustrated at having lost a potential sleeping partner!

She made herself look at him coldly. 'What do you want me to say? That I'm running from a broken heart? That I don't want to be hurt again?' she charged derisively, and saw his head go back as the words struck home. She told herself she couldn't have hurt him. He had to care to be hurt, and he didn't care. He didn't!

A muscle flexed in his jaw. 'Either, if they're true,' he returned grittily, and Megan shook her head.

'They're not. The truth is no man has hurt me. They can't. I'm more likely to hurt them. I'm trying not to hurt you, Lucas.'

'Why?'

The soft challenge shook her to the core. 'Wh-what?'

Lucas smiled grimly. 'It's a simple question, darling. Why don't you want to hurt me? You've never worried about the others, have you?'

Her mouth went dry as she saw where his clever brain was taking him. She wouldn't go down that road. She dredged up a likely explanation. 'No, but I've always considered you a friend, Lucas. That's why I don't want to hurt you.' She waited for his reply. It wasn't long in coming.

'I don't believe you.'

She hadn't counted on such a blunt denial, and it left her floundering. He wasn't responding the way he should. He read things into what she said that shouldn't have been there. The man defied all logic! Alarm skittering along every nerve, she saw red. 'Damn you!

Why can't you just be angry like a normal human being?' she cried, and he had the gall to laugh.

'Is that what you want?' he asked silkily, and her nerves screamed.

'It's what I expected,' Megan shot back, crossing her arms defensively when she saw the speculative gleam grow in his eyes.

'Well, sweetheart, you got what you expected, because I am angry, though not in the way you think. I'm not angry for the things you've done, but for the things you won't do. You say you don't want to hurt me, and yet you won't trust me. *That* hurts me, Red.'

Megan felt a ball of emotion swell inside her. There was no doubting his sincerity, but she didn't want it. Couldn't take it and what it implied. Yet, loving him, she was discovering how much it hurt her to hurt him, and she felt compelled to compromise. Her throat worked like crazy in order to allow her to speak. 'I do trust you, Lucas. You know I do.'

Lucas took the few steps necessary to bring them face to face, and took hold of her shoulders. He shook his head. 'Not in the ways that count. For God's sake, I can feel your pain. Share it with me, Megan.'

The plea very nearly broke her. How could he know the agony she suffered? She had hidden it all these years, and nobody had ever suspected before. Lucas seemed to know so much. He offered comfort she hadn't realised she needed until now. Yet old habits died hard. She didn't want his pity. The secret must stay locked inside her.

She wasn't aware just how much of her anguish showed on her face, but Lucas saw, and with a muffled oath he brought his mouth down on hers. For Megan the world shut down. She was rendered defenceless by the tingling pleasure of his lips teasing hers, and when she opened them the silken stroke of his tongue plundered with devastating need. She could not deny him what she needed so badly herself, and for vital seconds she responded, rising on tiptoe to press herself against him as the kiss deepened to fever pitch.

Then Lucas's hands tightened, pushing her away, and she stumbled backwards, fingers pressed to her throbbing lips. 'Why did you do that?' she croaked, licking her lips and tasting him there, instantly wanting more.

'Because your eyes begged me to,' he answered equally huskily, and she looked away in dismay, aware that one kiss had undone a thousand words. 'Don't worry, I'm not about to leap on you. I'll leave you alone for now. Just don't think this is over. One way or another, there will be truth between us.'

With those words of warning, he ran a gentle hand down her cheek and across her lips, before abruptly turning and walking away.

Megan watched him go with an anxiously beating heart. Nothing had turned out the way she had expected. Lucas had implied that his feelings for her were more than simply sexual, but it couldn't be true. Whatever it was, it wasn't love. He couldn't love her. He just wanted her and hated being thwarted. Yet if he loved her... No! She couldn't think that way! Lucas did not love her! He never had and never would. She didn't want him to. It wouldn't bring her joy. It would be the worst possible thing to happen. She could cope with anything but that.

Dropping down to the grass again, she hugged her knees up to her chest and wrapped her arms around them. 'Please, God, don't let him love me,' she prayed over and over in a litany of despair. She didn't cry, but, physically and emotionally exhausted, she stretched herself out on the soft turf and closed her eyes against the sun. She welcomed its warmth easing over her like a blanket. Without realising it, she slept.

* * *

Hours later she woke. The sun had moved round, leaving her in dappled shade, and she sat up, feeling slightly chilled. A glance at her watch told her it was the middle of the afternoon, and she scrambled to her feet, heading back along the path to her car. Lucas's Jaguar had gone, and she wondered where he was. Almost immediately she told herself it didn't matter. She had no business thinking about him. They would soon be going their separate ways, and she would have to pick up the pieces of her life.

She drove home, bracing herself to face Lucas again, but his car was missing, although her brother's was parked outside. Daniel didn't answer to his name, though, when she went indoors, and she presumed they must have gone somewhere together. She hoped it boded well. She didn't doubt that Lucas would know what to do.

She forced herself to eat a sandwich she didn't want, then took herself into the garden to spend the rest of the afternoon weeding. The sun had already gone down by the time she stopped, and the only interruption had been Ted ringing to tell her he was going out to dinner. Wearily she made her way upstairs to shower, then changed into a large baggy T-shirt and grey leggings over a frivolous pair of silk panties. She was just fastening gold studs in her ears when she heard the sound of a car and knew the two men had returned.

She found Daniel in the lounge. He was sitting on the couch, his legs propped up on the coffee-table. Glancing round tensely, she realised he was alone. 'I thought I heard Lucas,' she remarked casually, feeling anything but casual. Sitting beside him, she curled her legs up under her.

Daniel stretched luxuriously. 'You did. He's gone through to the study. He said he had a call to make,' he explained genially, causing her brows to lift questioningly. When he said no more, however, she was forced to prompt him.

'Well? What happened?'

Daniel tried to keep his face straight, but it was impossible. Giving in, he gave her the wry smile he used always to have. 'Lucas came up trumps, Meg. Just like you said he would.'

Megan felt her heart swell at the knowledge that she hadn't been mistaken. 'He said he would help?'

Daniel let out a relieved breath. 'He already has!' he exclaimed wonderingly. 'I nearly bolted, I was so ashamed of myself, but I knew I had almost ruined you as well as myself, so I had to speak out. Lucas was marvellous. He didn't criticise, just listened to what I had to say, then asked me how much I needed.'

Megan felt light-headed with relief. 'Just like that?'

Daniel looked sheepish. 'Well, not exactly. He said he thought a thrashing might do me good, but that as you wouldn't like it he'd agree to help with my debts providing I seek proper counselling. I know I've been a fool, Meg, but I'm not such a fool that I don't know when I need help. I jumped at the chance. I need to get my head together if I'm going to square things with you. First, though, I've got to get Terrell's back on its feet.'

Megan frowned. 'I thought you were going to sell Terrell's?'

'Lucas doesn't think it's a good idea. Rather than selling, he says we need an injection of cash. He suggested he becomes a partner; that way he can supply the money, and I can pay both of you back out of my share of the profits.'

Megan didn't know what to say. Lucas's generosity was breathtaking. She had expected him to help, but not to go that far. He was taking an awful risk. She couldn't imagine why he had done it. 'And you agreed?' she asked unnecessarily.

'Did I! This is just what we need. Terrell's can be
great, Meg, but it will take hard work. That's my fault.
I should never have let things slip so far. But I'll make
it up to you, I promise.'

Megan bit down hard on her lip. Daniel was no saint.
She knew he would keep his word about the gambling,
but he was too restless to stay here and slog away at
rebuilding the business. He had to be up and doing,
and she couldn't see them competing with the best for
some time to come.

Before she could venture any of what she was
thinking, Daniel spoke again. 'By the way, you've got
another commission. Lucas wants you to design a boat
for me to race. That way I can promote Terrell's the
way it deserves. We're going to be up and running in
no time, Meg, and I can't wait!'

Though it did her good to see the enthusiasm return-
ing to her brother, her head was reeling from all the
plans he was telling her about. All of them inspired by
Lucas.

As if by magic he appeared in the doorway, looking
far too handsome in a blue silk shirt and white chinos.
A cut-crystal glass holding some golden liquid nestled
in his palm, whilst his other hand was slipped casually
into a trouser pocket.

'Well, children? Is God in his heaven and all right
with your world?' he drawled ironically, running an eye
over Megan, which set her heart thumping. Without
waiting for an answer he drained his glass and set it
down on the nearest table. 'I won't be in for dinner, so
you two will have to celebrate on your own. Don't
drink too much, Dan. The holiday is over, remember.'

A second later he was gone. They heard his car start
up, the noise fading as he drove away.

He left behind an uneasy silence as brother and sister
looked at each other.

'I don't know what's the matter with him,' Daniel

declared, frowning. 'He's been acting out of character all afternoon. Usually he has great concentration, but today his mind has been elsewhere. Has he said anything to you, Meg?'

'No,' she lied, well aware of where his thoughts had been. On her.

'Well, I'd say it was a woman. What's the betting old Lucas has fallen in love, and the woman of his choice is playing hard to get?' Daniel laughed, though not unkindly.

Unfortunately it was too close to her secret fears, and Megan got to her feet jerkily, nerves all on edge. 'Don't be silly. You know Lucas plays the field.'

Daniel shook his head, his expression serious. 'Not since he got here, he hasn't. In fact, the only woman I've seen him with is you.'

Her heart leapt into her throat and she turned on him angrily. 'If you make the stupid suggestion that Lucas is in love with me, I swear I'll hit you, Daniel!' she warned fiercely, taking him aback.

He held up his hands. 'Hey! I haven't said anything. Besides, what would be so wrong with that?'

Watching the possibility cross his mind and find approval, Megan felt angry, helpless tears stinging the backs of her eyes. 'Everything would be wrong with it! Can't you see that? It would be... It would be...' She couldn't finish the sentence, and, pressing her lips tightly together, she crossed to the window and stared blindly out.

Daniel gaped at her back in shock and growing understanding. He'd never seen Megan so uptight. 'You're in love with him, aren't you?' he asked gruffly, though he knew he didn't really need her answer.

Megan gritted her teeth. Emotions seethed inside her, so that it hurt to breathe. 'Lucas does not love me,' she said firmly, but naturally Daniel did not understand that she was trying to convince herself more than him.

'I think you're wrong, Meg. It wouldn't surprise me if Lucas did love you. Come to think of it, he's always had a soft spot for you, right from when we were kids!' He sought to reassure her, to give her the hope he thought she needed, unaware that it was the very last thing she wanted to hear.

A bubble of hysteria broke out of her, and she laughed achingly as she turned round. 'Don't you understand? I don't want him to love me! I don't want anyone to love me! I couldn't bear it!'

Daniel stared at her. 'But. . .if you love him. . .?'

'I want him to love anyone but me.'

'That doesn't make sense, Meg!' Daniel protested, floundering.

She smiled tiredly. 'Yes, it does. Oh, yes, it does,' she countered thickly, and took a deep breath. 'Now, if you don't mind, I'd rather not discuss it. Just tell me what you want for dinner.'

Daniel looked as if he wanted to argue at the abrupt change of subject, but in the face of her determination he was forced to bite the words back. 'I've lost my appetite. I think I'll go and do some work in the study.'

Megan bit her lip as she watched him go to the door. 'I'll make you a sandwich. You might get hungry later,' she said softly, and he glanced at her over his shoulder.

'I don't understand you, Meg.'

She blinked back tears. 'I know. You'll just have to trust that I know what I'm doing.'

Daniel shook his head in defeat and disappeared, leaving Megan to bury her face in her hands. What on earth was she doing, ranting at Daniel like that? She was falling apart. The whole fabric of her life, so painfully built up, was dissolving before her eyes. All because she loved Lucas.

Yet love had never been an option for her, so why

did it hurt so to cut him out of her life, when she had always intended to do so? Her heart had the answer her mind could never have seen. She loved Lucas. A living, breathing man, not an abstract idea. To deny herself something in the abstract was easy; to deny the reality was like ripping out her heart. She had never thought it would be so hard, but it was, and the longer it took, the harder it was. This morning had been difficult enough. She had the distinct feeling that if she didn't get Lucas to accept that whatever had been between them was over, and soon, she would shatter into a million irretrievable pieces.

Which meant she had to try again. Tonight, when he came home, she would be waiting for him. This time she would succeed. She *had* to succeed. To envisage anything else was unthinkable.

The hours passed slowly, with nothing holding her interest on the TV. Eventually she went up to her room, curling up on the window-seat to wait until Lucas returned. She hadn't intended to sleep, but she must have, for something woke her with a start, and, glancing at her watch, she discovered it was almost midnight. Sitting up, she listened, just faintly hearing the sound of a door closing. It had to be Lucas, for Daniel had gone to bed before her for a change. Clambering stiffly from the seat, she ran her fingers through her hair and let herself out into the corridor.

Lucas's room was at the other end of the hall, and when she reached it there was no light showing under the door. She debated going away again, but was reluctant to leave the matter hanging. If Lucas was asleep already, he would just have to wake up.

For the first few seconds after she entered the darkened room Megan thought it was empty, but when they probed the gloom her eyes finally picked out Lucas's figure stretched out on top of the bed, his shoulders propped against the headboard. What faint light there was caught the glitter in his eyes and told her he was looking right at her. Closing the door, she leant back against it.

'I have to talk to you,' she said firmly.

'Naturally it couldn't wait until morning,' he responded, and she heard the mocking amusement behind the words.

'No,' she confirmed, aware, now that her eyes were getting used to the dimness, that Lucas wore a towelling robe and probably nothing else. It was a distraction she could well have done without. All she could do was ignore it—no easy thing when everything about hin drew her like a magnet.

'So tell me, what is so important that it brings you hotfoot to my room in the witching hour, at great risk to your reputation?' Lucas went on drily, and Megan gritted her teeth, knowing he was taking devilish delight in drawing the moment out. She raised her chin, determined to keep her cool.

'First I wanted to thank you for helping Daniel. You were more than generous.'

Lucas drew one leg up and rested his arm on his knee. 'He's my oldest friend. You knew I wouldn't let him down,' he said simply, and even in the gloom Megan felt her eyes lock with his.

Her heart kicked, and she had to moisten her lips with her tongue in order to carry on. 'Yes, I did know, but even your loyalty has limits. I never expected you to offer to become a partner, or commission the boat for Daniel to race. I appreciate it, but I don't understand why you went to those lengths.'

'Don't you?' he challenged her softly.

Megan's skin prickled at the waves of energy coming from him, and she realised it had been a mistake to come. She should have waited until morning. But it was too late to back out now, so she forged on. 'I know you have a good heart, Lucas, but—'

'But nothing,' Lucas interrupted immediately. 'I didn't do it out of the goodness of my heart, Red. I did it for you.'

The simple statement stunned her defenceless heart. 'For me?'

'I know just how important Terrell's is to you,' he replied, and Megan caught her breath.

For a moment she thought he really did know, but she got a grip on her anxiety when logic told her he was simply speaking generally. However, he had made her too edgy to stand still, and she pushed away from the door, taking several steps into the room. 'Naturally. It's been in the family a long time.'

Lucas shook his head. 'It goes beyond that. For some reason I have yet to discover, Terrell's is your life. And I find that a strange thing to say of a woman who has so much more to offer,' he declared thoughtfully.

The words found targets he had no conception of, and she winced, glad of the shielding darkness. The laugh she forced past her lips was ragged. 'You know that's not true,' she said edgily.

Lucas did not laugh. 'No, I don't know. You've got me turned inside out, so that all I really know right now, this minute, is that I need you.'

Her heart constricted at the words. It was unbelievable how much pain could be caused by something which was supposed to bring only joy. Next to 'I love you', they were the words a woman most wanted to hear, but to Megan they spelled only horror. Her composure was shot to pieces. Needing someone implied an emotion beyond caring, and that plunged her into her worst nightmare She didn't want to hear this. She had to stop him before he said anything more. Before he said words which would explode in their faces.

'Now listen, Lucas, you have to stop this!' she

protested shakily. 'It's not funny any more. We both know you don't need me!'

'Oh, but you're wrong; I need you very much,' he declared huskily.

Oh, God! She curled her nails painfully into her palms. 'What you're talking about isn't need, it's plain old-fashioned lust!' she decried, willing him to retreat and not drive her to say things she would always regret.

In the next instant shock waves chased along every nerve as Lucas swung his feet to the floor and closed the gap between them. She took a half-step backwards then forced herself to retreat no further, biting back a moan when she felt his hands close on either side of her head, tipping her face up to his.

'It's never been that, for either of us. You know it; that's why you keep trying to deny it. I know it frightens you, but, honey, you aren't the only one. I've never felt this way before either. You feel it the same as I do. Feel it!' he ordered throatily, and she didn't have to try because already that electric charge was passing from his flesh to hers.

When his head lowered, a whimper of despair forced its way from her throat. His mouth found hers, lips scorching with the faintest caress, barely touching and yet possessing her very soul. She wanted to sink into his embrace and never surface. Heaven was here for the taking, but it had the sweetness of hell.

'I don't want this.' She forced the necessary lie from an achingly tight throat.

Lucas uttered a sighing laugh. 'You do,' he murmured, trailing a line of kisses along her jaw and up to her eyes, which closed as if they were weighted. 'Just give in to it, Red. I'll keep you safe. I swear it.'

His closeness made it incredibly difficult to think just when she most needed to be clear-headed. 'You have to stop doing this!' she protested once more.

'It would be easier to stop breathing than to stop

wanting to make love to you,' Lucas declared with a groan.

Megan shivered, staring up into midnight-dark eyes which invited her to drown in them. She felt as if knives were being driven into her heart. 'Don't make me hurt you, Lucas,' she pleaded thickly.

'You're going to have to do your worst, Red, because, like it or not, you're the woman I want,' he said softly, and she caught her breath.

Megan felt the burn of tears behind her eyes. 'This wasn't supposed to happen!' She was supposed to be fighting, rejecting him, not clinging as if she would die if she let him go!

Lucas paused, pulling away enough to be able to look at her, and her heart ached when she saw the tenderness in his deep blue eyes. 'Wasn't it? Remember, I told you in the beginning you couldn't dictate to love,' he breathed, and lowered his head.

This time his kiss was a sensual ravishment. He allowed her no space to retreat, plundering and claiming her mouth with blatant hunger. Megan felt an answering need well up inside her. For sanity's sake she tried to quell it, yet it was inevitable that she should fail.

It hurt too much to refuse herself what her tortured heart cried out for. She knew she would live to regret it, that she would pay a high price for stealing these moments, but she was willing to pay it for a few more hours of the joy that only Lucas could give her. With a muffled sob she capitulated, sinking against his strong body, sliding her arms helplessly up around his neck and burying her hands in his hair.

At the same time his arms enfolded her, holding her close, letting her feel for herself the power she had to arouse him. It was heady and exciting, and her mind and body claimed him. Right or wrong, he was hers! And, as if he had been able to hear that silent assertion,

Lucas dragged his mouth free of hers and gazed down into her molten eyes.

'You're mine, Red,' he declared huskily.

Megan closed her ears to words of caution. She didn't want to think. 'Yes,' she sighed back. For tonight she would be his. Tomorrow. . . Tomorrow would look after itself.

He ran the ball of his thumb over her bruised lips, making her eyes close. 'What, no fight?'

Her lids rose up; her eyes were a seething caldron of emotions. 'Don't let me think, Lucas. Make the night last for ever!' she beseeched, and his lips curved.

Lucas bent to swing her up in his arms. 'Anything for you, Red. You have only to ask,' he declared thickly, carrying her to the bed and lowering her gently on to it.

CHAPTER NINE

THERE was a moment when Megan awoke when she felt quite blissfully happy. She sighed and shifted her head on the pillow, a slow smile beginning to form.

'When you look like that, is it any wonder that I love you?'

The smile vanished and her eyes shot open. Lucas was lying on his side, his head propped on his hand. His hair was mussed, he was gloriously naked, and he was waiting for a response.

For the moment Megan was blessedly numb. 'What did you say?' A pained whisper was all she could form in a throat as tight as a drum. Lucas had been as good as his word—he had allowed her no time to think last night—but she was thinking now, and she knew the time of reckoning had come.

Lucas smiled at her, misinterpreting her shock. 'I said, I love you,' he repeated simply, lowering his head to brush his lips over hers.

Megan twisted her head sharply, so that his kiss fell on her cheek instead. She felt him tense, then ease away to look down at her. She couldn't look at him, not yet. The numbness began to evaporate. 'You don't know how much I wish you hadn't said that,' she murmured in distress, and his hand came out to capture her chin, using gentle force to turn her to face him.

The tension in him was tangible, but the only sign on his face was the nerve ticking in his jaw. 'I was hoping for a different reaction.'

Emotion deepened the green of her eyes, for she knew she must put an end to this, and there was no way to do it without causing pain. Yet she had to do it, and she hardened her heart. 'You didn't seriously expect me to say I loved you, did you?' she challenged mockingly, wishing he would let her go, because his gentleness was surely killing her.

Lucas's nostrils flared as he took an angry breath. His eyes flashed and his smile was grim. 'Why not? It wouldn't be the first time,' he responded shockingly, calling her bluff, and her eyes widened in dawning horror.

Dear God, no! 'You couldn't possibly. . .!' she cried, appalled.

'Oh, yes, I was awake,' he told her tersely, keeping a tight rein on his anger and watching the colour drain out of her.

'No!' Megan denied desperately, thrown on the defensive though all her weapons had been effectively stripped from her in one telling blow. She sat up, moving as far away from him as the bed would allow, searching for something to cover her nakedness. There was only the pillow, and she clutched it to her like a shield.

Lucas sat up too, a wry smile twisting his lips. 'You can't hide from me any more, Megan. I won't let you, no matter what you say to try and make me angry or change the subject. I was awake when you came out of the bathroom. I heard you tell me you loved me, but I also heard your fear. I didn't understand it, but I knew you needed time. So instead of revealing that I wasn't asleep I gave you that time. Only to discover when I did talk to you that you'd gone into full retreat.

'I didn't know why then, and I still don't. Even after a night spent making love to each other, you were prepared to deny it, if you could. But I'm not going to let you. I love you, Red, and I know you love me. I want to hear you admit it.'

Breathing raggedly, Megan stared at his, trying to think although her brain had turned to mush. 'Why? It won't change things,' she countered tightly, feeling a wild trembling start deep within her. She had to get out, and her eyes gauged the distance to the door.

Lucas shook his head. 'You'll never make it, but you can try if you like,' he said levelly, and when she didn't move he took a deep breath. 'OK, now tell me what sort of things won't change.'

He had her trapped, and though he looked relaxed she knew he wasn't. He was prepared for anything, and that included getting some answers. Well, since he had asked, she would have to tell him. 'I don't want you to love me,' she ground out painfully, and immediately Lucas shook his head.

'It's too late for that, Red. It was too late the moment I saw you again.'

She looked away, biting her lip against the pain of words which tore her heart apart. She could feel him willing her to open up and let him in, but she couldn't do it. 'Then I want you to stop loving me,' she ordered jerkily.

'Sorry, no can do,' Lucas replied bluntly, bringing her head round again.

'But you have to!' she cried, eyes shimmering with lashed tears. 'I can't bear for you to love me! I'd rather you hated me!' Because hate would cauterise the hurt, and she *would* hurt him.

The softening of his blue eyes stole her breath away. 'I'm sorry, Red, but I can't do that. I intend to keep on loving you until the day I die,' he informed her with such gentleness that it brought a sob of despair to her lips.

'Don't say that!'

'It's the truth, and the truth can't hurt you, Red,' he countered.

It could! It was driving a stake through her heart. Megan felt the trembling intensify until she could barely control it. She knew she had to get away before she broke down completely. 'I can't take any more of this!' she exclaimed in anguish, and leapt from the bed. Lucas was right behind her, catching her before she reached the door and hauling her into the prison of his arms. She fought him wildly, but he was much too strong, and finally she collapsed against him, panting for breath.

'What are you so afraid of? What is so awful about having me love you?' he demanded, his breath brushing her ear as he spoke.

Megan looked up, seeing beyond his anger to the pain in his eyes, and it was a like a dagger in her soul. The fight went out of her. She wanted to cry, and closed her eyes against the sting of tears. 'Because I'll hurt you, the way I'm hurting you now,' she confessed in a cracked whisper. 'Please, Lucas, just let me go,' she begged.

He took a deep breath, not denying her claim, but he didn't let her go. 'No. I want to know. Don't you see, I *have* to know? I've been waiting for you all my life. Do you honestly think I would give you up without a fight?'

Megan pressed a hand to her trembling lips. No one had ever spoken to her with such a depth of emotion, and it was as beautiful as it was deadly. He was baring his soul in an attempt to get her to trust him, unwittingly giving her weapons to hurt him with. And she would have to hurt him, because he wasn't going to back down, not this time. A whimper escaped her. 'You expect too much of me, Lucas!' she croaked, praying for numbness to take away her own pain, but knowing it would not come.

The passionate blue eyes locked on her distressed green ones. 'Because I want you to love me?'

'But that's not all, is it?' she groaned. He had told her what he wanted when he met the right woman. It was everything she wanted him to have, and everything she could never give him. 'Don't you want to marry me? Have a f—' Her voice broke, and she willed herself to go on. 'Have a family?' she finished faintly, desperately wishing he would let her go, because it was a refinement of torture to be held so close.

Lucas tensed as he sensed her agitation. 'Naturally,' he confirmed cautiously.

Megan would have given a fortune not to go on, but there was no turning back. Knowing it, suddenly she felt a strange calm steal over her, distancing her. There was nothing she could do to avoid the outcome he insisted on, so he could have his truth, even if it destroyed them both.

'Natural to you, maybe, but not to me. I don't want those things.' Her tone was flat, unnatural, and he frowned down at her.

'But you love children. I saw that for myself,' he countered, and she winced.

'I've told you more than once that I don't want children,' she reminded him coldly, and he eased away from her a little, trying to catch her eye but she refused to look at him.

'A lot of women say that, but they change their minds,' he pointed out, quite truthfully. It happened, but not to her.

'I won't change my mind,' she declared, and Lucas uttered a grim laugh.

'You might have to,' he said shortly, and she stared at him blankly.

'What do you mean?'

'Hasn't it occurred to you? We've made love several times, without any thought of protection. You could already be pregnant,' he informed her, and she could tell that part of him hoped she was.

Megan laughed, but it was harsh and painful, totally without humour. Of course it hadn't occurred to her because she knew it couldn't happen. 'No, I could not be pregnant. I've been on the Pill for years, and have no intention of coming off it.'

That, finally, made him release her, and she felt instantly chilled. Rubbing her arms, she spied her T-shirt in a heap on the floor and retrieved it, slipping it over her head with relief. Clothed she felt less vulnerable. Taking a deep breath, she turned to face Lucas and found him frowning at her.

'Even for me?' he demanded tersely. Careless of his nakedness, he looked handsome and proud, and Megan hoped his pride would get him through, because he had given her an opening she could not refuse.

'There are definite limits to what I will do for love,' she declared bluntly. She produced a faint smile. 'So there's no risk of the dreaded patter of tiny feet. For which I am heartily grateful,' she lied. It had never been easy, and never would be.

Lucas didn't seem to know what to say. Shaking his head, he dragged both hands through his hair then automatically picked up his robe and pulled it on, tying the belt with restrained anger. Megan watched him sadly, wanting to offer comfort but knowing she couldn't. When he glanced her way, she quickly summoned a smile and a shrug.

'And, as you know, I've never been a candidate for marriage. It would stifle me.'

He stared at her as if she had suddenly grown another head. 'Yet you say you love me,' he said tautly, and she sighed.

'I told you I didn't want to hurt you, Lucas. Yes, I love you, but I don't want the same things you want. I'm sorry,' she said huskily, and took a step towards him.

He held up a hand, palm out, to ward her off. 'Thanks, but I don't want your pity!' he snapped disgustedly. 'I don't particularly care for your brand of love either.'

Megan turned away on the pretext of picking up the rest of her clothes. Her hands were shaking so much, it was a wonder she managed it. She felt dead inside. Finally, he believed her, but she had had to hurt him to achieve that and she would never forgive herself for that. Straightening, she licked dry lips and prepared to drive the final nail into the coffin.

'You'll get over it. You might think you love me now, but you won't tomorrow. When you give yourself some time to think, you'll come to the conclusion you never loved me in the first place.' She couldn't say any more. The words would choke her. Squaring her shoulders, she headed for the door.

'What about you?' His question halted her with her hand on the knob. She didn't turn around, so failed to see the arrested look on his face. 'Will you still love me tomorrow?' he asked in the strangest voice.

I'll love you for ever, her heart replied. 'Oh, I've a very fickle heart, but maybe I'll love you till the next man comes along!' she quipped, and made her escape.

Outside she collapsed against the wall. The old saying was right: you could take what you wanted, but you had to be prepared to pay for it. She was paying for last night. She should not have stayed, but she had wanted to steal a little more time. Now she had for ever to remember that she had destroyed something fine: Lucas's love.

Uncomfortable with her guilt, she straightened and continued on to her room. Sinking onto her dressing-table stool, she dropped her head in her hands. What an awful mess her life had become. In the space of a few short days she had broken all her rules. She had thought she knew what heartache was, but nothing compared to this.

A tear trickled down her cheek, but she brushed it away and pushed herself to her feet. She didn't have time to break down now. In a few hours she would have to face Lucas again, and nothing of the misery she felt must show on her face. She just had to keep telling herself she had done the right thing. She had left him free to find someone who could give him all the things he wanted—things he deserved, because he was a kind, loving, honourable man, who had had the misfortune to fall in love with a woman who, through no fault of her own, must deny him that most precious of gifts—a family of his own.

It was almost nine-thirty when Megan went down to breakfast. She had gone through the motions of showering and dressing in fawn trousers and a green silk blouse. She had felt the need for make-up too, to give her face some much needed colour. A glance in her mirror had shown her a virtual ghost. She felt as ephemeral as one, too. Her spirit had been beaten down until now she was running on empty. It felt as if it wouldn't take much to crush her altogether.

She had hoped to find the kitchen empty, but when she pushed open the door she found Lucas seated at the table, lingering over a cup of coffee. Her instinct was to retreat, as her heart twisted painfully, but then she stiffened her spine. She wasn't a coward and she had made her choice. She wasn't about to back out, so the sooner she got used to meeting Lucas, the sooner her defences would strengthen. One day she might even be able to face him without that deep sense of loss.

He hadn't noticed her yet, and she found herself studying the top of his head. It was funny how vulnerable it made him seem, and she had the urge to go and run her fingers through the silken strands soothingly. She couldn't, though. Such automatic signs of affection were strictly forbidden if she was to hide her feelings from him. He must be given no reason for supposing she had lied.

Still as she was, she must have made some noise, for he suddenly looked round, spearing her on the end of a hooded glance. Then, to her utter surprise, for it was the last thing she ever expected, he smiled. To her beleaguered spirit, it was as if the sun had come out inside her. It was simple and beautiful, and yet it hurt more than anything ever had. She could not have spoken if her very life had depended on it.

'Good morning. I still don't suppose I can interest you in a marriage? No? Then how about a cup of coffee? You look as if you could do with one.'

Megan made it to the nearest chair and sat down abruptly, knocked sideways by his disconcerting behaviour. 'Wh-what. . .?' she managed to mumble incoherently, and Lucas smiled wryly, poured her a cup of coffee from the pot in front of him, and set it before her. She stared at it as if it might explode. Thrown off balance, she had no idea what was going on.

Lucas appeared to have no such problem ordering his thoughts. He spoke as if they were discussing the weather. 'I suppose you realise you are the only woman I will ever marry?' he said softly, and Megan stared at him incredulously. How could he have said that? They had been through this.

She turned her gaze blindly to the coffee in her cup. 'You'll find someone else,' she declared thickly.

'It's you or no one, Red,' Lucas returned doggedly, and her stomach lurched.

She stared at him, eyes glittering with anger and a boundless hurt. 'Why are you doing this? I thought. . .' The words tailed off painfully.

Lucas relaxed back in his chair, his intent gaze never leaving her. 'You thought it was over? Unfortunately for you, I have a good memory.'

Megan couldn't seem to draw her eyes away from his. Like a rabbit caught in the headlights of a car, she could only wait for the moment of impact. 'And what is it you think you've remembered?' she charged, feeling rushed and trapped and totally unaware that it showed in her eyes.

Lucas saw, and his jaw clenched briefly before he sighed and climbed to his feet. Walking round the table, he came to a halt behind her, setting his hands on the back of her chair, making her tense. Ambivalently she found herself torn between not wanting him to touch her and dreading that he wouldn't! Her skin began to burn with the reflected heat of his, and she shivered as his nearness sent tingles chasing along her nerves. She wanted to lean back against him. To close her eyes and breathe him in. God help her, she was such a mess!

His voice broke into her despairing thoughts. 'I remembered what you said after your date the first night I was here. You'd just broken off with him, and you said he didn't love you, but that even if he did he wouldn't tomorrow. Does that sound familiar?' he enquired softly.

Megan closed her eyes, recalling those words all too clearly and realising the enormity of her mistake. She hadn't expected him to put two and two together like that. She had forgotten how dangerous he was. 'That doesn't mean anything,' she denied shakily.

'Then why are you trembling?' he asked, hands shifting from the chair to her shoulders, thumbs rubbing back and forth in a rhythmic movement which started flash fires on her skin.

'I—I'm cold!' she lied, then wished she'd remained silent for she was burning up and he knew it. He knew exactly what his touch did to her.

'Uh-uh. I think you're afraid, Red. Afraid of what I might find out. And you should be, because I'm not giving up. I'm never going to give up on you,' he told her huskily, bending to press a kiss to the top of her head.

Megan shuddered with a mixture of pleasure and horror. She jerked away. 'You have to!' she insisted raggedly, rising on unsteady legs and turning to face him. He was expressionless, tensed to do battle for as long as it took.

'Why?'

'Because I say so!' she shouted back, then, alarmed by the wildness inside her, she caught her breath and walked over to the sink, gripping the edge like grim death. 'You have to let me go, Lucas. Oh, why can't you be like other men, who would walk away without a thought?'

'Because I'm not like other men. I'm the man who loves you,' he told her simply.

Her knuckles grew white with strain. 'It wouldn't be enough.'

'Enough for what?' he asked her quietly, and Megan took a shuddering breath.

'To stop me hating myself,' she replied, and, straightening her spine, turned around. 'That's why you have to stop this. We both know you could wear me down, make me give in, but I'd still end up hating myself. I'm begging you not to go on.'

Lucas stood watching her without saying a word until she felt like screaming. Finally he sighed. 'I'll tell you what I'll do. I'll make a deal with you. All you have to do is tell me the truth. The complete, unvarnished truth. Then, and only then, will I walk away,' he proposed evenly.

Tears stung her eyes. He was asking the impossible. 'I can't,' she denied thickly, and Lucas breathed in deeply

'You're a stubborn woman, Red. If I didn't love you so much, I'd probably throttle you. I'm going out before I give in to temptation. But don't worry, I'll be back. You can count on it!'

He went out, leaving Megan feeling as if she had

gone fifteen rounds with a heavyweight boxing champion. Lucas would not give up. How painfully ironic it was that the measure of his love for her was the very thing which was hurting her. Yet she couldn't tell him. She had her pride, and she did not want his pity. Somehow, there had to be a way to make him stop before it was too late.

But what?

The telephone rang out in the hall, and Megan took a steadying breath before going to answer it.

'Hi, Megan, it's Peggy. I thought you might like to come over for coffee. Jack's taken the boys fishing, so there's just me and the baby. We can have the whole morning to ourselves.'

Megan found the idea instantly tempting. To get away from the house for a while would be wonderful. There would be no chance of running into Lucas, either, because he would be working with Daniel. 'OK, I'll come.'

'That's marvellous!' Peggy declared in relief. 'You remember the way? Good. I'll see you in about an hour, then. Bye.'

Megan put the receiver down slowly. Thank goodness for Peggy. She was a life-saver. More than that, she could be an ally. If anyone had influence over Lucas, Peggy did. If she could only get her onto her side, perhaps Peggy could persuade Lucas to give up this dangerous game he was playing.

Encouraged by the thought, Megan quickly cleared up the kitchen, collected her bag and car keys, and headed out the door. She had no difficulty finding the Lakers' cottage, and her spirits had improved noticeably by the time she pulled up outside the gate. Peggy was there to greet her, a gurgling Annie in her arms.

'I'm so glad you could make it. The children are marvellous, but it's nice to have a conversation with an adult now and then!' she joked, slipping her arm casually through Megan's as they made their way round the house to the patio.

Megan made herself comfortable on one of the loungers set out there whilst Peggy put the baby in her shaded baby seat before coming to join her.

'How are you, Megan? I have to admit to being worried about you after you left,' Peggy confessed.

'I'm fine,' Megan instinctively replied, then sighed tiredly. 'No, that's not exactly true. I'm ashamed of myself for creating such a scene. It was very rude of me.'

'Nonsense. Where can you have a scene, if not with friends?' Peggy dismissed easily.

Megan studied her hands. 'Yes, but you're Lucas's friend, not mine.'

Peggy frowned at the younger woman's lowered head in concern. 'I hope I can be a friend to both of you,' she said gently.

Licking her lips, Megan gave Peggy a shaky smile. 'I was rather hoping you would say that, because I have a favour to ask of you,' she said gruffly, clearing her throat nervously.

Peggy tipped her head curiously. 'Yes?' she invited, and Megan sighed again.

'I want you to persuade Lucas to get out of my life,' she declared scratchily, holding onto her composure with some difficulty.

'But, Megan. . .' the other woman began to protest gently, and Megan reached out swiftly to clutch at her wrist and halt the refusal she knew was coming.

'You must! If you're his true friend, then you must do this for me. You have to tell him it's in his own best interest!' she insisted hardily, unaware of just how deeply her fingers were biting into the other woman.

Peggy ignored the pain doggedly. 'But is it?' she asked, her lips parting on a tiny gasp as Megan tensed.

'Oh, yes!'

'I can't pretend to know what's going on, but I can't help feeling this is wrong. You love each other,' she protested worriedly.

The claim brought a frown to Megan's brow, and she released Peggy's abused arm abruptly. 'How do you know that? Have you seen Lucas?'

Peggy rubbed at her arm automatically, and shifted uneasily in her seat. 'He. . .telephoned. He sounded very upset.'

Megan set her jaw. 'That's all the more reason for you to do this for me. He refuses to let me go, no matter what I say. You'll have to persuade him that he must.'

Peggy's troubled gaze never left the younger woman. 'I can see it means a lot to you, Megan, but I can't be expected to persuade Lucas to do something without knowing why. I have to understand why you want this. Can't you tell me that?'

Megan stared at her, caught between the need for help and the reluctance she had always had to reveal the truth to anyone. Yet Peggy was her last and best hope. Her heart thudded sickeningly.

'If I agree to tell you, you have to promise never to repeat what I say to another living soul,' she demanded huskily.

Peggy caught her breath and, out of sight, crossed her fingers tightly. 'Of course I promise. I won't tell anyone.'

Still Megan hesitated, swallowing to moisten a tight throat, feeling emotion roiling inside her. 'I've never told anyone,' she began awkwardly. 'I swore to myself I never would. But it's the only way, isn't it?' She sought confirmation with cloudy emerald eyes.

It was impossible for Peggy to remain unmoved by that look, and her face softened into a smile. 'You don't have to say anything if you don't want to,' she advised gently, and Megan shook her head.

'No. I've got to tell you because I need your help. Everything has gone so wrong. I never meant to fall in love with Lucas, and when I did I tried to end it without hurting him. He won't listen. He just keeps telling me he loves me, and it's me or no one. Even though I've told him I don't want children, he refuses to accept it. He's leaving me no choice but to tell him I can't have them!' she exclaimed despairingly, not hearing Peggy's gasp of shock. 'Lucas loves children.'

'I always say he wants a football team of his own!' Peggy responded, her voice wavering disastrously on the verge of tears.

Megan's bottom lip trembled betrayingly, and she pressed it tightly to the other. 'Well, I can't give them to him. The thing is, I know he'll say he can accept that, but I can't! Oh, it would be so easy to give in, to take what he offers, but I'd never forgive myself. With another woman he could have that football team! I *want* him to have them! I've never seen a man more suited to have children, and he deserves them, Peggy,' she added huskily, looking at the other woman through glittering eyes.

Peggy reached out and captured Megan's hand. 'Are you sure you can't have children? There are so many tests these days, so many ways of achieving the impossible,' she said unevenly, and Megan dropped her eyes.

'You don't understand. I told you I can't have children, but the truth is, I can, but I won't.'

Peggy froze. 'I. . .you. . .'

Megan removed her hand, clutching it with the other in an attempt to stop it shaking. 'I have what they call a genetic disease. My mother had it, but I didn't know that until after she died. It's passed on through the female line, but it's only harmful to boys. When I heard. . .'

She paused, swallowing hard to conquer the emotion rising in her. 'You can't imagine what it's like to know you will condemn your own children to the same horror you feel. To know that your daughters will suffer the agonies you do. To live with the knowledge that they, like you, will have to watch their sons die before the end of infancy.

'I couldn't do it. No matter how much I long to have children of my own—and that's all I ever really wanted, you know—I couldn't do it. I couldn't do to them what has been done to me. I decided I had to be the one to end the chain of misery. Call it playing God if you want, but I don't regret my decision. I won't have children. I won't inflict heartbreak where there should have been love.'

'Oh, dear Lord!' Peggy's exclamation was the merest thread of sound.

Megan wiped at the tears which were slowly and silently trailing down her cheeks. 'It was easy to decide never to marry either. I wanted to avoid the pain of yearning for things I couldn't have. It was working, too, but, like a fool, I didn't allow for falling in love.

'Then this morning Lucas told me he loved me, and... It hurts, Peggy, knowing I can't give him what he needs. So it's got to end, only I can't tell him why because I don't want his pity! I couldn't live with that! And I'm so afraid he'll persuade me to marry him, but if I stay with him I'll just hurt him more. He'd have this great big emptiness inside him, all because of me, and I couldn't take it. So you see, you have to persuade him to let me go! You just have to!' she ended desperately, and finally dropped her head in her hands and cried as if her heart would break.

Beside her, Peggy stifled her own tears behind her hand. Looking towards the house, she stared into Lucas's pale, strained face, helpless to know what to say or do. He came over to her and she clasped his hand. 'You heard? Oh, Lucas, what an awful, awful thing...!' She shook her head in distress.

Lucas stroked her cheek. 'Take Annie inside,' he said softly, and as she did so he walked round to sit on the edge of Megan's lounger, reaching out to pull her into his arms.

She stiffened at once, recognising the scent and feel of him. She looked up, her face an agony of pain and betrayal. 'No!' she cried hoarsely, struggling to be free, but he caught her face between his hands and held her eyes with his.

'Don't fight me, Megan,' he ordered in a voice choked with tears. 'As you love me, don't fight me any more,' he added in a whisper, and drew her into the loving shelter of his arms.

She could not move then, for even to breathe hurt beyond measure. He had heard. He knew everything, and now there was nowhere for her to hide. She tensed at the feel of his hand smoothing her hair, feeling her last fragile defences crumble into dust.

Lucas breathed in deeply, trying to absorb some of her pain. 'Oh, Red, Red, how on earth could you think I would pity you, when I think you're the bravest woman on this earth?' he groaned.

Megan caught her breath, her fingers clutching the material of his shirt. 'You can't think that!' she challenged, and a laugh escaped him even as he closed his eyes.

'You'll have to get rid of this habit of arguing with me, darling. I do think it, and it's true. You're brave and proud, and quite helplessly fat-headed!'

That jerked her out of her cloud of despair. Her head came up at once. 'What?'

Lucas's smile was still shaky, but it was a smile. 'Only a fat-head would think I would chose marriage with a woman I didn't love in order to have children, because the woman I did love had made the heartbreaking decision not to have any of her own.' His hand slipped into her hair and cupped the back of her head. 'Don't you see, sweetheart? If I can't have you, I don't want anyone else. Speaking selfishly, I'd rather be childless with you than without you.'

Her eyes swam. 'How can you say that?'

'Because I love you,' he groaned, and brought his mouth down on hers in a kiss which stole her soul from her, but gave her his in return. When he drew away, her tears were gone, replaced by a look so defenceless that he felt like crying himself. 'I kept trying to tell you that you hurt me more by not trusting me. That is the only way you can ever hurt me.'

Megan reached out to press trembling fingers to his lips in mute apology. 'It wasn't a case of not trusting you, Lucas. I love you so much, I just want you to be happy. No matter what you say, you want children. You know you do!' she insisted.

Lucas sighed, brushing his lips across her forehead. 'Not being able to have children with you will be a sorrow, but it isn't the end of the world. We'll have each other—if ever I can get you to agree to marry me!'

Megan bit her lip. He made it sound so easy, so simple. 'But will it be enough for you?'

'Will it be enough for *you*?' he countered softly, and she blinked at him.

Strangely she had never thought of that. She hadn't wanted to hurt him. Had wanted to see him happy. She had never asked herself if she could be happy with him. It was a sobering thought, when she had always sworn that, if she couldn't have it all, then she'd rather have nothing. Years ago that had been true, but she knew it wasn't now. If only she could be sure that Lucas was happy, truly happy, then sharing her life with him would be all she would ever want.

'Oh,' she said at last.

Lucas started to laugh as some of the enormous tension left him. 'Why is it I never get the response I expect from you?' he asked wryly, and Megan felt an answering smile start to curve the corners of her mouth.

'Because I'm a contrary creature. You'll just have to get used to it,' she said softly, releasing his shirt to run her hand caressingly over the silky material, feeling the strength of him beneath it.

He stilled her hand by catching it in his and bringing the palm up to his mouth. 'How much time do I have?' he asked throatily, kissing the tender flesh and curling her fingers around the spot protectively.

Megan felt her heart expand as she finally allowed hope to enter. Maybe they had a future together after all. 'How does for ever sound?' she breathed, and the gleam in his eye was all the answer she needed.

'Sounds good to me,' he responded, drawing her close and closing his eyes on a wave of relief. 'Does this mean you're going to marry me?'

Megan lifted her hand to run the backs of her fingers over his jaw. 'Oh, yes, though I shouldn't. I'm just beginning to realise you set me up!'

He caught her hand and pressed it to his heart. 'What else could I do when you'd left me no choice? You wouldn't explain what was going on. I was desperate. All I could think of was getting you worked up enough to talk to someone, and Peggy agreed to help. Neither of us expected to hear what we did! It tears me up to think of you bearing all that on your own all these years. I wish you'd told me.'

Megan sighed wistfully. 'I didn't know I loved you then. I was afraid of anyone pitying me. I didn't want that. I would have taken my secret to my grave if you hadn't forced it out of me.'

'Forgive me,' he said gruffly. 'I never meant to hurt you. I just remembered seeing your face when you held Annie, and other times too, when you looked so sad. I knew you were hurting, and I wanted to ease your pain.

All I ever wanted was for you to trust me enough to let me help you.'

She had been blind, in more ways than one. 'I had no idea. I thought you were playing some devilish game of your own. I got used to fighting my own battles.'

'Not any more. You have me now, Red. Whatever happens, you know I'll always be there for you. I love you so damned much, your happiness means everything to me. Don't shut yourself off from me ever again,' Lucas ordered, and she had to smile.

'I won't, I promise,' she confirmed huskily, reaching up to seal the promise with a kiss.

He drank from her lips until they were both breathless, then pulled away to smile down at her. 'You drive me out of my mind. Lord knows what I'm letting myself in for!'

Megan let out a gurgling laugh and made herself more comfortable against him. 'Does that frighten you?'

With a laughing groan, Lucas caught her and pushed her backwards so that she was pinned underneath him. 'Hell, no! Whatever it is, it's going to be good.'

Megan smiled as he kissed her. She liked the sound of that. Liked the sound of it very much indeed.

EPILOGUE

MEGAN glanced up from the paper boat she was making as she heard the car drive up to the house. Her heart lifted instantly and a smile curved her lips. She looked over to where her son and daughter were splashing about in their paddling pool.

'Daddy's home!' she called out, and immediately the splashing stopped as, with squeals of delight, they abandoned the water for the greater pleasure of greeting their father.

Megan laughed as she watched them go, knowing Lucas would end up soaking wet but also knowing he wouldn't mind. He loved getting into a mess as much as they did! A scratching at her leg made her glance down, and she pulled a rueful face, handing the boat to the infant who waited for it so patiently.

'Was I ignoring you, James? I'm sorry. Here you are, darling. Isn't it a lovely boat? Shall we show it to Daddy?'

'Da-da-da-da,' baby James gurgled in response, and she took it as a yes and picked him up, settling him securely on her hip as she went to find Lucas and the children.

As she suspected, he hadn't made it much further than the front lawn of the lovely old cottage they had moved into shortly after their marriage. His briefcase, jacket and tie were strewn haphazardly in his wake and he was on the grass, tickling the life out of five-year-old Amy, whilst four-year-old Jonathan was clinging to his back like a rodeo rider.

Her heart swelled as she heard him laugh just before he collapsed and the two whirling dervishes piled on top of him. She had never dreamt that she could be so happy, and it was all due to Lucas. He had been the one to suggest adoption. Maybe they couldn't have babies of their own, he had said, but there were children out there just crying out to be loved. She hadn't needed much persuasion. Freed of her own nightmares, she had seen that they didn't have to be childless. There were other ways—good ways—for them to have the family they both wanted.

That was how they had come to get Amy and Jonathan. They had been an orphaned brother and sister who had stolen Megan's heart the minute she'd seen them. The love that she and Lucas had given them these past two years had made them blossom into the boisterous pair who had easily accepted the arrival of baby James, whom they had adopted six months ago. They were a lively, happy family, something Megan had never expected to be part of.

Seeing Lucas's hair caught in insistent fingers, she winced and went to rescue him. Dancing blue eyes met hers as she knelt down beside the giggling group.

'Do you know how much I love you, Lucas Canfield?' she asked with a grin.

'Enough to rescue me?' Lucas suggested breathlessly, reaching up with his free hand to tousle James's vivid red hair.

'You don't need rescuing, you love it!' she declared blithely, and gasped as he caught hold of her T-shirt and began pulling her towards him.

'Not nearly as much as I love you, Megan Canfield,' he breathed against her lips.

'You'd better not look. Daddy's going to kiss Mummy,' Amy pronounced, quickly putting a hand in front of her brother's eyes.

'Yuck!' Jonathan exclaimed with a toothy smile, and the pair of them fell about laughing whilst Lucas proceeded to do just that, very satisfactorily.

'Happy?' Lucas asked seconds later, sitting up to take James from her.

'Very happy,' Megan confirmed, welcoming Amy into the curve of her arm, whilst Jonathan tried to make a whistle out of some grass. Her heart was full. Everything she had ever wanted was right here, and the man responsible for it all sat with his children about him, making grass whistles. Later, when the children were in bed, and they were finally alone, she would make sure he knew just how very much she did love him and always would.

JUST ONE NIGHT
Carole Mortimer

Hawk Sinclair—Texas millionaire and owner of the exclusive Sinclair hotels, is determined to protect his son's inheritance.

Leonie Spencer—bruised by her own unhappy experience with marriage, is determined to protect her twin sister's happiness.

Hawk and Leonie are together for just one night. For Hawk no other woman would feel right in his arms again. For Leonie, hope flickered, and died that night. That night their daughter was conceived.

An international top selling author with over 50 million copies of her books in print, Carole Mortimer's inimitable style is loved the world over by romance fans.

MIRA®

MILLS & BOON®

Weddings ✣ Glamour ✣ Family ✣ Heartbreak

Weddings By De Wilde

✣

Since the turn of the century, the elegant and fashionable DeWilde stores have helped brides around the world realise the fantasy of their 'special day'.

Now the store and three generations of the DeWilde family are torn apart by the separation of Grace and Jeffrey DeWilde—and family members face new challenges and loves in this fast-paced, glamourous, internationally set series.

For weddings, romance and glamour, enter the world of

Weddings By De Wilde

—a fantastic line up of 12 new stories from popular Mills & Boon authors

OCTOBER 1996

Bk. 1 *SHATTERED VOWS* - Jasmine Cresswell
Bk. 2 *THE RELUCTANT BRIDE* - Janis Flores

Available from WH Smith, John Menzies, Volume One, Forbuoys, Martins, Woolworths, Tesco, Asda, Safeway and other paperback stockists.

GET 4 BOOKS AND A SILVER PLATED PHOTO FRAME

Return this coupon and we'll send you 4 Mills & Boon Presents™ novels and a silver plated photo frame absolutely FREE! We'll even pay the postage and packing for you.

We're making you this offer to introduce you to the benefits of Reader Service: FREE home delivery of brand-new Mills & Boon Presents novels, at least a month before they are available in the shops, FREE gifts and a monthly Newsletter packed with information.

Accepting these FREE books and gift places you under no obligation to buy, you may cancel at any time, even after receiving just your free shipment. Simply complete the coupon below and send it to:

MILLS & BOON® READER SERVICE, FREEPOST, CROYDON, SURREY, CR9 3WZ.

No stamp needed

Yes, please send me 4 free Mills & Boon Presents novels and a silver plated photo frame. I understand that unless you hear from me, I will receive 6 superb new titles every month for just £2.10* each postage and packing free. I am under no obligation to purchase any books and I may cancel or suspend my subscription at any time, but the free books and gifts will be mine to keep in any case. (I am over 18 years of age)

P61E

Ms/Mrs/Miss/Mr _____

Address _____

_____

_____ Postcode _____

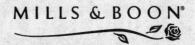

MILLS & BOON®

Next Month's Romances

Each month you can choose from a wide variety of romance with Mills & Boon. Below are the new titles to look out for next month in our two new series Presents and Enchanted.

Presents™

BEST MAN TO WED?	Penny Jordan
THE MIRROR BRIDE	Robyn Donald
MARRIED TO THE MAN	Ann Charlton
WEDDING FEVER	Lee Wilkinson
RECKLESS FLIRTATION	Helen Brooks
HIS COUSIN'S WIFE	Lynsey Stevens
A SUITABLE MISTRESS	Cathy Williams
CARMICHAEL'S RETURN	Lilian Peake

Enchanted™

WITH HIS RING	Jessica Steele
THE MARRIAGE RISK	Debbie Macomber
RUNAWAY WEDDING	Ruth Jean Dale
AVOIDING MR RIGHT	Sophie Weston
THE ONLY MAN FOR MAGGIE	Leigh Michaels
FAMILY MAN	Rosemary Carter
CLANTON'S WOMAN	Patricia Knoll
THE BEST MAN FOR LINZI	Miriam Macgregor